# SHADOW IN RED

A false charge of kidnapping a child brings together Cate Lindsay and Detective Inspector Adam Stone. Despite this proving to be a hoax, Cate finds herself embroiled in a dangerous game of cat and mouse with a devious impersonator who seems determined to ruin Cate's business. Unsure of who to trust, she tries to prove her innocence and uncover the perpetrator on her own, but finds she needs Adam's professional help — and also the love and support he offers . . .

SHEILA LEWIS

# SHADOW IN RED

*Complete and Unabridged*

LINFORD
*Leicester*

First published in Great Britain in 2006

First Linford Edition
published 2007

British Library CIP Data

Lewis, Sheila
    Shadow in red.—Large print ed.—
Linford romance library
    1. Impersonation—Fiction
    2. Love stories 3. Large type books
    I. Title
    823.9′14 [F]

    ISBN 978–1–84617–830–6

Published by
F. A. Thorpe (Publishing)
Anstey, Leicestershire

Set by Words & Graphics Ltd.
Anstey, Leicestershire
Printed and bound in Great Britain by
T. J. International Ltd., Padstow, Cornwall

This book is printed on acid-free paper

# 1

Cate Lindsay put her shopping bags on the kitchen table and shrugged off her red cape, glad to be home again. She considered whether she should have her meal now or press on with the work waiting for her on the computer. The shopping trip had been a necessary mid-day break. There was just so much work to catch up with, even a year after Max had gone off and left her to clear up the mess.

Debating whether to begin cooking herself some mushroom risotto, her eye was caught by two cars manoeuvring for a parking space on the road outside. Her kitchen window faced on to Croft Road and she watched with not a little irritation as the cars neatly boxed her in.

'Thanks a bunch,' she muttered to herself. Still she wouldn't need the car until the next day when she was due to visit her sister, Sue, and family. The cars would probably be gone before then.

She took the kettle to the sink, deciding to have a cup of coffee before doing either of her two options. People were emerging from the cars. A man and woman from the first, and three men from the other. She was struck by the fact that they all seemed to resemble one another in age, around thirty she hazarded, dressed in clothing which was dark and under-stated. It was possible they were council officials of some sort.

She'd just switched on the kettle when her entrance buzzer sounded. She lived on the first floor of an old Victorian house, long ago divided into flats. Of the four flat owners, she was probably the only one at home at this time of day, so she'd better see what they wanted.

'Miss Lindsay?' the male voice on the entry phone was business-like. 'Police. Can we come up?'

'Yes, of course,' Cate's stomach did a few somersaults and then she pressed the entry button. Police meant something was wrong. An accident, perhaps? Her thoughts flew to her parents who lived in Stirling, then to Sue and family who lived not far away in a small village. But did it take five people to inform her of an accident?

Even more apprehensive, she opened the door to the flat to find all five crowded outside and evidently not waiting for an invitation to enter.

'Detective Inspector Stone,' the man in front said and displayed his warrant card.

Cate held open the door and they all surged in over his next words, introducing the woman as Detective Sergeant Paterson, and the other three men as Detective Constables whose names she did not catch.

Her living-room wasn't all that spacious and suddenly it was filled to capacity.

'Is there something wrong? An

accident, my parents?' her voice rose with anxiety.

'This doesn't involve your parents,' D.I. Stone said. He was a few inches taller than her five-foot-seven height, with thick fairish hair, cut rather short. He had a broad face, but his features were contracted into tension.

Relief was only temporary as she noticed that the woman detective had gone into the kitchen, while one of the men was heading for her bedroom. 'Just a minute, what are you doing? What is going on?'

'You're just returned from Easiway supermarket?' the Inspector asked.

It was the last question Cate expected. 'Yes.' How did he know that?

'We've had a report of an incident there and we want to speak to you concerning that,' he said.

'An incident? You think I've stolen something?' She was horrified.

At that moment the woman sergeant came back into the living-room. 'Got it, Guv,' she said and over her arm she held Cate's red cloak.

The Inspector nodded at her and then turned back to Cate. 'A woman answering your description was seen leaving the Easiway supermarket with a baby in a pushchair,' he said.

'Well, it wasn't me,' Cate told him. 'I don't have a baby.'

'The baby didn't belong to the woman who took him,' Sergeant Paterson said.

'Well, as you can see I don't . . . ' then the reality hit her. Someone has taken, snatched, kidnapped . . . a baby . . . and they thought it was her!

'I didn't take any baby,' she said. 'Why have you come here?'

'The description given to us by a witness described you, in particular the red cape. I take it you were wearing that when shopping?' D.I. Stone asked.

Cate nodded. She felt as if she was stepping into a nightmare.

'And have a look at this, guv,' one of the constables had now emerged from the kitchen and was holding out a bag of shopping.

With horror Cate realised it was the baby food she'd bought to take to her sister's the next day. She always took a few bits and pieces for her nephew, James, and since she was babysitting she'd have the pleasure of feeding him, too.

'That is for my nephew. I'm baby-sitting tomorrow,' she said flatly.

'Doesn't his mother provide his food?' the sergeant's tone was heavy with sarcasm.

'Yes, these are extras,' Cate said. She knew it sounded weak, but how could she explain to these strangers the overwhelming love she felt for James and how Sue indulged her in letting her spoil him occasionally.

'What have you done with the baby, Miss Lindsay?' The Detective Inspector now asked.

'I don't have the baby,' she said, glaring at him. 'Look everywhere you want, you will not find a baby here.'

'Believe me we will, that's our job,' he snapped at her. 'We have information that someone has taken a baby without permission and we intend to find that baby before it comes to any harm.'

Cate suddenly thought of James and how she would feel if he had been taken away from his parents, Sue and Rob. The enormity of the frightening situation overwhelmed her.

'Nothing here, guv,' one of the men reported to the Inspector.

'Search the other flats,' the Inspector told his men. 'Break down doors to get in if necessary.'

'There's no need for that,' Cate cried, stopping the officers in their tracks. 'We all have keys to each others' flats in case of emergency.'

She went into the kitchen and collected the keys from her little wooden key cupboard on the wall.

She passed over the bunch, then felt her legs give way and she sank on to her sofa.

'And your car keys, Miss Lindsay,' Inspector Stone said and then turned to his sergeant. 'Check the boot of her car.'

Cate gasped. Did they think she would put a baby in the boot of a car? She picked up her red cape and took the car keys from the pocket. She handed them over to the woman.

Despite herself, she went over to the window to watch Sergeant Paterson unlock her car. She watched as the woman detective pulled up the boot lid and reached inside. Seconds later, she withdrew her head and looked up at the window, guessing her boss would be watching. She shook her head and slammed down the boot lid.

'Tell me what you were told and by whom,' Cate turned to the Inspector who'd remained with her, clearly making sure she didn't make a run for it.

'It was a call from a female, sounding hysterical, who told us that a woman answering your description, height, colouring, etc. but specifically wearing a red cloak was seen pushing the baby in a buggy away from the supermarket to your car. It was a pretty comprehensive account,' he finished.

'How did you know it was me?' she asked.

'The witness took a note of your car registration. We are able to trace owners with that information.'

'I have not taken any baby, Inspector,' Cate said carefully. 'That is a most horrific crime in my book. I don't know what I can do to make you believe me, but I do think you are wasting time here when the baby could be in danger elsewhere.'

'Don't presume to tell me my job, Miss Lindsay.' A flash of cold anger crossed his features. 'Somewhere there must be a mother frantic with fear and worry. I'm doing exactly what she expects me to do.'

'Who was this witness?' she asked.

'She rang off before identifying herself.'

'Really!'

'People do that in panic and when time is of the essence,' he told her.

At that point the officers returned to Cate's living-room. 'Nothing, guv. Flats are empty,' one said. 'Maybe she passed the baby on to an accomplice before we got here.'

'So what have you done with the child?' Stone whipped round to face her and she jumped back in fright, knocking over a vase of tiger lilies. She started at the sound of glass shattering.

'I didn't take the child!' she almost screamed at him, her nerves at breaking point, guessing though that it could sound like panic to him. 'I don't know what you are talking about. I didn't even see a child in a buggy at the supermarket, let alone take it away.'

Stone's blue eyes were cold as granite as they searched hers as if weighing the truth of her claim. 'I have no alternative but to ask you to come to the police station,' his voice was flat and he turned away to nod at Paterson.

She grabbed Cate's red cloak from the sofa and thrust it at her.

'But why? I've done nothing!' Cate protested again.

'We have a witness who saw you take a baby from the supermarket,' Paterson repeated the accusation in a relentless monotone.

\* \* \*

Downstairs, Cate was put in the back of the Inspector's car with Paterson sitting beside her.

Numb with fright and the inability to prove she had done nothing wrong, Cate sat motionless during the journey, unable to register what was happening or where the journey was taking her.

Sergeant Paterson kept a firm hand on her arm as she escorted Cate into Ashrigg's police headquarters. Inspector Stone disappeared once inside and Cate was left at the desk to give the officer there her personal details and the contents of her handbag. Then Paterson took her to an interview room.

Cate couldn't believe this was happening to her. She had the sensation of being a viewer watching a scene in which she had no part. She felt incapable of any protest, any reaction, any feelings.

Then Sergeant Paterson came into the room and set up some cassette tapes. The Inspector arrived a few minutes later and they took chairs across the table from Cate.

'Do you want to have your solicitor present?' the Inspector asked.

For a second Cate panicked. Her brother-in-law, Rob, was her solicitor, but there was no way she wanted the family involved! She would deal with this on her own. Marshalling all her spirit, she responded to the Inspector.

'Why? When I haven't done anything?'

Stone shrugged his acceptance of her refusal and he began questioning her, going over the same ground again and again. All her shopping had been brought to the station, even food destined for her freezer and she watched mutely as the packets began to defrost and become soggy, spreading a puddle on the table. What was the point of that?

As if reading her mind, the Inspector

turned to his sergeant. 'What's all this food doing here? Take it away.'

Suddenly Cate had had enough. She put her palms flat down on the table and leant over to face the Inspector.

'Yes, I wondered that too. What kind of evidence is there in frozen food?' she swept on, conscious she had his full attention. 'Let's get the facts clear. You tell me that you have a witness who claims she saw me taking a child in its buggy from the supermarket. She gave you a description of me with particular reference to my red cloak,' she pulled it round from the back of the chair where she'd placed it. 'And she even gave you my car registration.'

Inspector Stone had not taken his eyes from hers and she saw his expression flicker, but could not gauge what he felt about her outburst.

'So why didn't she stop me? Why didn't she shout for help at the time? Why did she wait until, she claims, I had put the baby and the buggy in the car before contacting you?'

Stone's blue eyes looked away for a moment, but not before she thought she saw a shadow of uncertainty there. She was about to follow up her advantage when Paterson jumped in again.

'You want a baby, don't you, Miss Lindsay?' Her eyes were hard. 'The old body clock ticking?'

'How dare you!' Cate began.

She observed an irritated flick of the Inspector's fingers in his sergeant's direction. He clearly didn't approve of that line of questioning.

'Miss Lindsay,' he said. 'I have to think of parents out there in agony because their baby has gone missing. I have to know what's happened to it.'

Cate began to wonder how long she could maintain a steady façade. She was determined not to show how weary, and indeed frightened, she was. She had to keep calm until they finally realised she had not taken the child and started to look for the real kidnapper.

'I didn't take any baby. I don't know

where it is,' she repeated in a monotone.

At that moment there was a knock on the door and a uniformed policeman entered the room. Paterson took a whispered message from him and then relayed it, in similar fashion, to her boss.

The Inspector followed the policeman from the room. Cate kept her head down, hoping Paterson would not go on the offensive again, but to her surprise she said nothing.

Shortly afterwards, Paterson was summoned from the room. Common sense told Cate that there must have been some development. But what if it was something else to falsely incriminate her?

She had to fight hard to resist an overwhelming urge to slump on the wooden table. Her body felt as if it had all the strength of a rag doll. She clasped her trembling hands in her lap in an attempt to still them. Her nerves were screaming out to be told what was happening.

Then she was aware that the Inspector had returned to the room. She didn't look up but guessed he was alone, there was no sound of other footsteps.

'You are free to go, Miss Lindsay,' he said leaning over towards her. 'We now know you did not take any baby.'

Cate raised her head then. 'The baby is safe? Thank God,' she burst out and felt tears flood her eyes, partly for the child and his parents and partly from her own relief. 'Is it all right?'

The Inspector's eyes held hers. 'While we were interviewing you another team was at the supermarket to ascertain what had happened. There were no reports of any baby being snatched, no distraught mother. Nothing. No-one has phoned us to report any kidnapping today.'

Cate stared at him.

'Miss Lindsay, I'm more sorry than I can say that we had to put you through all this, but as soon as we received that phone call we had to act. It's imperative in baby kidnapping cases that we find the child as soon as possible before any harm can befall it.'

'But what does all this mean?' At last Cate managed to talk.

'It means that you and we have been the subject of an elaborate hoax.'

'A hoax?'

'I'm afraid so,' his tone was now gentle and caring. 'I know this has been very distressing for you and I can only apologise. We get people doing this all the time. People who confess to crimes they didn't commit, who make hoax telephone calls to us, as this person did today. These people are ill, an illness that they sometimes can't control. They want attention, to feel important for once.'

Cate rose wearily from the table, her limbs stiff and painful.

'I'll drive you home, Miss Lindsay,' the Inspector said at once.

'There's really no need,' she replied with automatic politeness.

'It's the least I can do after putting you though such a gruelling time.' He took her cape from the back of the chair and draped it round her shoulders. 'I'm off duty now.'

'Well, yes, I would be grateful to be taken home,' Cate said, realising she was exhausted.

She collected her belongings from the front desk. 'As she put her mobile phone back in her bag, the Inspector made another apology.

'I'm afraid we had to take details of incoming and outgoing calls on your phone. The record of those will be destroyed.'

Cate nodded, not caring, just relieved it was all over.

He led her to his car and as he opened the passenger door, he said: 'I'm Adam Stone, by the way.'

'I'm Cate Lindsay,' she said in response, then stopped with her hand on the door. Surprising herself, she laughed. 'Of course, you will know that, how silly of me.'

They got into the car.

'Not silly, just a symptom of the

trauma you've endured today.' He smiled at her.

She was suddenly aware of him as a different person. For the first time she noticed his dark grey suit, the crisp white shirt and silk tie which had a clever geometric pattern. The planes of the face had somehow altered, making him look strong, yet no longer forbidding. As his eyes met hers she noticed they had reverted to their clear blue colour, their expression softer.

As he drove her home, he talked of the town and the changes it had seen over the last few years. Ashrigg was situated just north of the Scottish central belt, with easy access to both Edinburgh and Glasgow, but surrounded by acres of green.

The Campsie Hills to the south took the brunt of westerly rain but left the town at the mercy of northern winds and snows. Now, in mid-October, it was languishing in a warm mellowness, a typical late legacy of a Scottish Indian summer.

Gradually relaxing, Cate made her own comments on the civic developments and by the time they reached Croft Road, they had even found something to laugh about in the tiny sculpture of an igloo outside the frozen food shop.

He parked behind her Fiesta and said: 'I'd like to come in with you, if I may, just to make sure everything is all right. My officers didn't have time to tidy up after their search of your flat. We felt we had to move quickly.'

'I don't mind tidying up but perhaps you could explain to my neighbours why you had to enter their homes,' she said.

'Yes, of course, I'll do that.'

But first he came up to her flat. She was grateful for his consideration. It sounded ridiculous but she felt as if her privacy had been invaded earlier. Not just by the police, but by the anonymous caller who had led them to her.

Indoors, the sense of the earlier intrusion evaporated. Her own place seemed to welcome her with if not a sense of peace, at least of relief.

'This is a beautiful room, Cate,' he said, dropping the formal *Miss Lindsay*. 'I didn't take it in earlier.'

She watched as he studied the high decorated ceiling, so typical of Victorian architecture together with the gracious bay window from where she'd watched the sergeant search her car.

He looked at the painting on the wall that she'd bought in her parents' antique shop in Stirling.

In his wander round the room he'd now reached the door to her bedroom. 'May I just check things haven't been disturbed in here?'

She nodded.

'I'm afraid they've stripped the bed,' he said, returning almost at once. 'Shall I make it up?'

'No, I'll be fine. I'll do it later. Won't take a jiffy,' she assured him.

'You're absolutely bushed,' he said perceptively. 'I don't want to intrude on your personal life, but I think a cup of coffee would go down well. I make a rather good one.'

She realised he was trying very hard to make up for her horrendous afternoon, although she was certain it wasn't part of his job.

'I'd appreciate that, Adam,' she said his name quite deliberately too, hoping it would make him feel she held no grudge.

She leaned her head on the back of the armchair and heard him fill and switch on the kettle, was aware that he found the brush and dustpan and swept up the smashed vase and flowers.

The coffee was good and she told him so.

'All part of the better service.' He paused. 'I truly regret your ordeal and the manner of my questioning today, but it's the rules of the job, although I was certain you had not taken a child.'

She stared at him. 'Why did you think that?'

'I'm trained to observe character and all kinds of little gestures either give people away or reveal their honesty. Your first reaction was concern for your parents, so I felt you were a compassionate person and didn't seem the type to kidnap a baby. But I couldn't overlook the fact that there had been a witness.'

'Especially since that witness was so precise in her description of me,' Cate said thoughtfully. 'I can't understand how anyone could be so deliberately cruel.'

'Yes, it was deliberate and calculated. Without wanting to alarm you, can you think of anyone who might bear you a grudge?'

# 2

'A grudge?' Cate was stunned. 'You think someone thought up this hoax because they bear me a grudge?'

'I can't think of any other reason,' he said, sounding apologetic.

'I don't know anyone who would do something so heinous like this over a simple grudge.'

'It might even have been your distinctive cape.'

'Well, it is a one-off,' she told him. 'My sister had it made for me in Austria last year. A gift for being god-mother to her son.'

'It is beautiful and it does make you stand out in a crowd.' He smiled ruefully.

'Just my luck some crank spotted it today,' she said.

He leant over and touched her arm briefly. 'I've organised a statement for the local paper detailing this hoax call and warning the offender that she faces charges of wasting police time. We've already tried to trace the call — without success I'm afraid — but the publicity will scare her off and she won't trouble you again.'

'She'd better not,' Cate said stoutly.

'That's the spirit. Forget about today and enjoy the weekend. You don't have to work, do you?'

Cate shook her head. 'I'm going to visit my sister tomorrow so I have no alternative but to leave the office.' She smiled and pointed to her computer. 'That's my job.'

'What do you do?' he asked.

'Business packages. I have a list of clients.' She kept it vague.

'Good for you.' He picked up the tray.

'There's no need to tidy up, I'm fine now.'

'After a tense case like today's I like to do physical things, clears the mind and all that. I'm off tomorrow so I'm taking a hike along the Drovers' Path just outside town.'

'That's all of eight miles,' she exclaimed, knowing the local hikers' favourite route.

'Have you done it?' he asked.

'Twice.'

'Maybe we could walk it together one day. You could show me features of the trail that I might have missed,' he sounded hopeful.

'OK,' she said casually, but felt a frisson of pleasure.

★ ★ ★

Adam rose early next morning and prepared for his walk. He lived in a small flat convenient for police head-quarters and had furnished it with minimum fuss.

That was the professional side of his life. He had another residence, home he called it, but it was very private and well away from Ashrigg. He tried to keep the two parts of his life as separate as possible.

As he breakfasted, he stared at the slip of paper on the table in front of him. On it was written Cate Lindsay's mobile phone number. It wasn't quite a breach of regulations that he should have made a note of it from the record of yesterday's interview. On the one hand, it was only relative to that and the case was officially closed. It was highly unlikely that they would be able to trace the hoaxer.

On the other, he was uneasy about the crank's hoax. The hysteria in her voice had been faked and she'd been cunning enough to ring off without identifying herself. He felt sure that the hoaxer would either have been around the supermarket waiting for the police to arrive, just to see what havoc her call had caused or could have followed Cate home and watched the developments as he and his team arrived.

It was the accurate description of Cate's appearance, plus her car registration number that suggested to Adam that this had been a planned hoax with

Cate as the specific target.

Last night she had shrugged off any possible enemies and she certainly didn't seem the type to instil jealousy. In the time they'd spent together he'd formed the opinion that she was an upright, honest person, with a compassionate nature. There was also a strong streak of resilience in her make-up and he'd been glad when she'd challenged him over the details given in the hoaxer's phone call. She would not scare easily or consider herself a victim.

Although far more interested in character, he had to admit that she was also a most attractive girl. Her light brown hair had some natural auburn streaks and her green eyes were open and frank. A classic nose, a pretty mouth and a beguiling smile completed the picture. He admitted to himself that keeping her phone number was born of more than just occupational caution. It was a long time since he'd found himself so drawn to someone. Yet he didn't want her to be part of his professional life.

He dialled the number of her mobile. He wanted to know if she'd had a restful night. That was his excuse anyway. But he was unlucky. Her phone was not switched on.

★ ★ ★

'Why on earth didn't you phone and ask us to collect you?' Sue Douglas asked her sister when she arrived at Heronsfield.

'I didn't want to put you to any bother,' Cate told her. 'The bus was quite convenient.' She tried hard to make light of her journey. Tried hard to blot out the memory of what she'd seen at the bus station.

'You're not having to get rid of your car too?' Sue's voice was sharp.

'No. It just wouldn't start this morning,' Cate told her. 'You know I'm not technically minded so I just abandoned it and walked to the bus station.'

'You need a more up-to-date car. I don't suppose you can afford it at present. If you ask me that Max has a lot to answer for, swanning off, leaving you to shoulder that business on your own,' Sue went on, slicing a cucumber with unnecessary venom.

'That's all water under the bridge now,' Cate tried to keep the sharpness from her tone. Sue had no real idea of just how much Max Imrie had to answer for. She'd managed to hide all that from her parents and sister.

'Don't suppose you've heard from him,' Sue could worry a subject like a dog with a bone.

'No, I haven't and frankly I don't want to.' Cate lied. 'He's gone and that's that. I can assure you too, the business is doing just fine without him.'

Cate picked up her mug of coffee, determined to evade any other questions for as long as possible. She was saved by a wail from the garden.

'My nephew is calling me,' she told her sister and left the kitchen.

Her sister and husband lived on the edge of Heronsfield, a pretty village about fifteen miles from Ashrigg. Their house was in a small cul-de-sac and the rear garden bordered the Drovers Path which Adam Stone had mentioned yesterday.

Cate threaded her way through a jungle of toys in the conservatory and went out into the garden. Her nephew, Daniel, was sitting up in his pram, waving his arms and drumming his feet.

She laughed. It wasn't bad temper, just a demand for attention after his early morning sleep.

'Hello, gorgeous.' She undid the straps and lifted him out of the pram, planting a kiss on his soft hair.

Daniel's knees pumped up and down jabbing her in the stomach while he batted her face with joyful recognition.

'You'll have to go easy on the welcome stakes in a few years' time,' she told him. 'Some girls are delicate flowers.'

She put him down on the rug spread across the lawn and tickled him for a moment. She loved listening to his throaty giggle. In a minute or so he was grabbing some handy toys and soon became absorbed in examining those.

Not taking her eyes off him for a minute, Cate let her thoughts drift back to Sue's comments.

It was now over a year since Max disappeared from her life without warning. She'd met him several months before that when they both worked for an accounting firm in Glasgow.

Of mixed Scandinavian and Scottish parentage, Max was a typical Viking — tall, blond and devastatingly attractive. Despite that, she was loath to admit it, there was a streak of ruthlessness about him, although she hadn't discovered it until it was too late.

It was Max who suggested they leave the Glasgow firm and set up their own company in Ashrigg. They would provide business packages for small companies, even one-man businesses, who found it difficult to cope with all the paperwork involved.

Thus had Enterprise Expertise been born. Joint partners, she and Max supplied their clients with everything from accounting, to publicity, to seeking out new contacts, anything in fact that involved tedious form filling, or legwork, which distracted their clients from their dedicated professions.

Cate had invested all her savings in the company, but within months it had taken off. They took a let on a couple of small offices in Ashrigg's town centre. Cate felt fulfilled in her work for the first time since leaving university. Added to that, she fell in love with Max and he with her. At least she'd thought so, until that day when he just didn't turn up.

'Lunch is ready,' Sue called from the house, interrupting her thoughts.

Cate blanked out the past, scooped Daniel up from the rug and carried him indoors.

Her brother-in-law, Rob, had arrived back from his tennis match and gave his son a smacking kiss.

As they tucked into salad and Rob brought them up to date with all the lobs and serves which had won his game, Cate reflected on the atmosphere of happiness and tranquillity that dominated this household. There was no way that she would ever tell them what had happened yesterday, or even earlier this morning. Just as she had never told them the whole story of Max.

In the afternoon the three of them took Daniel in his buggy for a short stroll along the Drovers' Path.

Although chatting with ease to her sister, Cate found she was keeping an eye out for Adam Stone. He'd said he'd be walking the Path today. It had been such a relief when he'd stayed with her the previous evening. She had somehow felt completely at ease in his company, strange rather, after all she'd been through earlier at his hands.

Maybe he saw her as more than just another hoax statistic. She rather hoped he might, although the chances of meeting him again were probably very slim. Well, she'd wait and see if he ever did telephone her.

'You should keep that switched on,' Sue said. 'I thought business people always did that in case a millionaire was trying to contact them with a fantastic offer.'

Cate laughed. 'Chance would be a fine thing.'

Normally, she did have it switched on, but this morning she had forgotten, her mind still mulling over the previous day's happenings and Adam's comment about someone bearing a grudge against her. She could think of no-one. In fact, she was friendly with all her clients and had good working relation-ships with them.

She picked it up, switched on and then almost jumped out of her skin when the mobile beeped signifying it had a text message for her.

With a surprised thrill, she saw it was from Adam Stone. First he enquired if she was OK, then he suggested she buy the local paper where he'd placed a warning to the hoaxer.

She replied at once. *Fine, thanks. At my sister's today. Will get the paper when I return home tomorrow.* She almost signed off but then added. *Didn't see you on the Path today, cold feet?*

'Aha,' Rob leant back in his chair, watching her. 'Looking at that smile on your sister's face, Sue, I reckon it was a millionaire or,' he paused and grinned at Cate. 'A better offer?'

She jumped in immediately. 'Who was it, Cate? Have you met someone?'

For a moment Cate longed to say 'yes', but then that would lead to how and where and when and that was to be avoided at all costs.

'He isn't quite a millionaire.' She paused. 'But business is business,' she finished vaguely.

Two minutes later her phone rang.

'Hi,' she said in answer to Adam. She quickly left the kitchen and walked into the conservatory. It wouldn't do to let Sue and Rob hear her conversation. They'd soon guess it wasn't even a near-millionaire on the line.

'My sister lives in Heronsfield and we took a short walk along the Path this afternoon,' she said in reply to his enquiry.

'Too late,' he said. 'I was up there with the larks. You are OK though after yesterday?'

'Apart from being pummelled by a ten-month old nephew I have no complaints,' she said lightly.

She hugged to herself his last words. 'I'll call you tomorrow evening. OK?'

★ ★ ★

Next morning, after baby-sitting over-night at Heronsfield, Rob insisted on driving her back to Ashrigg.

'For one thing I can take a look at your car,' he told her as they had breakfast in the warm kitchen. 'It might be just a simple fault.'

'If it's anything more serious, I suggest you think about getting a new car, well a good second-hand one anyway,' Sue said. 'I like to think you're safe driving around the country.'

'Sure,' Cate said casually. 'I'll think about it.'

As she packed her overnight bag in the bedroom, she wondered if it would be a good idea to think about another car. After all, that hoaxer had her registration number. Then she dismissed that thought. Why should she go to all that expense? She wasn't going to be intimidated by some crank.

When she and Rob arrived back at Croft Road, he went straight to her car. Cate followed him, anxious to know if there might be some huge repair bill in the offing.

'Hey, your bonnet catch is loose,' he said at once. 'Did you forget to close it properly yesterday?'

Cate stared at him. 'I didn't even

open it. No point as I wouldn't have been able to spot anything wrong.'

'That kind of thing doesn't happen by accident,' he said, propping open the bonnet. He looked inside, fiddled about with some bits of the engine, and then turned to her.

'I think someone's been interfering with your car.'

# 3

The first thing that Cate heard when waking was the rain dripping off the eaves of the house. Why had it to rain today of all days?

She'd waited a whole week for this. It was Sunday again, but this time she was meeting Adam Stone. He'd phoned her several times now, each call lasting longer than the previous one, each of them somehow reluctant to break the connection.

Today they planned to walk the Drovers' Path. She slipped out of bed and drew back the curtains. Unrelenting rain washed down the windows. Just then her telephone rang.

'Hi,' Adam greeted her. 'I've personally instructed the sun to break through some time today.'

'Until then a little light drizzle doesn't matter,' she joked in return.

'That's the spirit. I've waited all week to see you, even a flood won't stop me now.'

'I'll see you soon,' she murmured, her heart fluttering at the intensity of his words.

She could hardly believe that she'd only met him once. That on such a brief acquaintance, he'd managed to break through the barrier of protection she'd set up after Max's abandonment of her. She had truly believed Max loved her until she'd received his e-mail on her laptop on the day he disappeared.

*Got an offer I can't refuse in Sydney. Good luck with the biz.*

No mention of love. No mention of the future they'd planned together. And she never heard another word from him. And the *biz* — their joint venture Enterprise Expertise — had overnight become her total responsibility. And he'd left that in the lurch too.

But now, after a year, she felt she was almost there in restoring it to financial security. When he dumped her, and she could think of no other description, her self-esteem had plummeted to an all time low. It was only the responsibility of the business that had eventually steadied her, but she had since avoided all personal involvements.

She put Max and the business firmly out of her mind and concentrated on getting ready for Adam's arrival.

Fifteen minutes later they were stowing wet weather gear in the boot of his car, laughing at the rain, daring it to spoil their day.

But half-an-hour into walking the Path, they knew the downpour wasn't going to ease up.

'Let's shelter under this tree for a moment,' Adam suggested. 'You're shivering.' He rubbed her arms as if to stimulate circulation. 'If I'm not being too forward, a hug might generate a little warmth.'

'Sounds like a good idea,' she murmured and slid her arms round his waist as he enveloped her in his arms.

They stood for a moment, her head

nestled against his shoulder, then he said: 'We have to get out of the rain. I know a short cut to the Inn.'

Sue and Rob had once taken her to the Drovers' Inn for lunch and she remembered it as a cosy pub.

Adam took her hand and led her through trees and scrub on a barely-marked path. Finally they emerged from the woods and found the Inn.

'Seems like we're not the first,' he said, gesturing at the full car park. There wasn't even a spare chair, never mind a table in the pub.

Back outside, they sheltered under the porch for a moment. 'We're not actually too far from my car. I know somewhere else that will be warm and dry. Shall we try for that?' he asked.

Soon they were back where Adam had left his car and they threw the wet gear into the boot.

To Cate's surprise, Adam headed the car away from Heronsfield and in the opposite direction to Ashrigg. Finally he turned off on to a farm track and drove down to its end. A low wooden fence surrounded a small stone cottage which nestled there, backed by some pine trees. A sign nailed to the gate said: *Owlsmoor*.

'I'll have a fire lit in no time and we can find something to eat from the freezer,' he said.

Cate stepped out of the car, enchanted by the cottage and its setting.

Adam opened the door and stood back to let her enter. She walked right into the main room and gave an involuntary gasp. It was a low ceilinged room, but light flooded in from long windows at the rear, illuminating the pale stone walls and the mellow wood of old furniture. Bright rugs covered the flagged floor and the soft furnishings were in shades of rust and soft blues.

'Adam, this is beautiful!'

'Yes, isn't it. It was my grandmother's home and she left it to me. I haven't changed it much. The furniture is almost all hers, I've just added some colour to the place, updated curtains and so on.' He walked over to the stone fireplace and set a match to the crumpled newspapers already laid under sturdy logs.

The light and crackling from the fire drew them both to kneel before it. 'I had no idea you lived out here,' she said.

'Ah, that's the rub. I can't live here and do my job properly so I have a small flat in Ashrigg. This is my bolt hole, if you like. Known to only a few of my friends and my family, of course, not anyone in the force. This is the private me.'

Adam went off to rustle up a meal, insisting he'd cope alone and she had time to reflect on the comforting fact that he'd brought her to his private place. She guessed few had had the privilege.

As she warmed her hands at the fire, she was glad she'd kept the worries of the last week to herself. Not for anything would she have told him about her car being vandalised, as Rob had put it. It hadn't been anything drastic, just a disconnected wire, and her brother-in-law had been able to fix it. She'd let him think it had been the work of vandals, but she was certain it wasn't.

When she'd found the car wouldn't start last Saturday, she'd walked to the bus station to catch the service for Heronsfield. As she'd been about to board, a flash of red had caught her eye. She'd turned round to see a woman hurry behind a neighbouring bus, but not before it registered with Cate that the woman was wearing a red cloak, trimmed with green.

She could not be sure in that quick glimpse, but it seemed that the garment was identical to hers. It had been an unnerving experience and she suspected it was no accidental sighting.

During the bus journey to Heronsfield she had calmed down and applied a sense of logic to the occurrence.

How would someone have known she was going to be at the bus station? Only if, surely, that person had been keeping her under observation since early morning. She would have seen Cate trying to start the car, then give up and begin walking to the station. And the unknown person had followed her.

Cate shivered at the knowledge that she was being spied on. But why? And why the copycat style of dressing?

It all sounded a bit fanciful in her opinion and she had decided not to mention the incident to Adam. It was hardly a crime to dress like someone else.

Adam returned with a tray. Two plates of lasagne emitted tantalising aromas and the glow from the fire enhanced the deep ruby of the wine in the glasses.

They sat cross-legged on the floor, eating at a low coffee table. 'This is such a peaceful place,' she told him.

'Mmm, the cottage has a rather special warmth. I'd like some more paintings. I noticed you had some rather good ones in your flat.'

'My parents have an antique shop in

Stirling and I'm afraid art is one of my weaknesses. I'm probably their best customer.'

'Maybe you'd take me there one day?'

'Of course. It's a bit chaotic as Mum runs it and she doesn't have a great business head. I help out with the accounts, otherwise they'd be broke,' she laughed.

Cate finished off her wine, and began to look around the room. 'You have some good photographs, Adam.'

'Photography is my hobby. If I'm ever chucked out of the force I might make a living taking holiday snaps on some beach.' He stood up to join her.

Cate walked round slowly looking at his collection. Some were of familiar Scottish scenes, depicted from unusual angles and he'd made use of seasonal light to great effect.

A family photo was next. The man was clearly Adam's brother, the resemblance was strong. A fair-haired woman stood beside him, with two young children in front of them, each holding children's surf boards. The background was the sea.

'My brother and family who live near Sydney,' Adam said.

Cate then picked up a photograph of a stunning girl with a perfect oval face, framed with thick dark hair which rested on her shoulders. It was a black and white print, very dramatic.

Adam said nothing for a moment. 'That was Ellie.'

'She's beautiful,' Cate said admiringly, not having missed the past tense in Adam's words.

'She was killed by a drunk hit and run driver,' he said baldly.

'Oh no!' Cate whispered.

'We'd only been going out a few weeks, but her death made me change my life.'

Cate waited.

'I was in local government in the legal department, but I decided to join the police. I wanted to do something more positive. The guy was eventually caught, but given only a light sentence because he had a clever lawyer.'

'Adam, that was tragic.'

'It was,' he agreed. 'It was six years ago and the pain has gone now, but the loss of a young life is unforgettable.'

★　★　★

It was late when Cate returned home, Adam dropping her at the flat. He'd had a call on his mobile to return to the station, so she slipped out of his car, after exchanging a brief kiss.

It hadn't been the first. That had come when dusk had crept up outside Owlsmoor cottage and they'd sat by the firelight, drawing closer and closer. It seemed natural just to move into each other's arms to make the first real physical contact with exploratory kisses — gentle yet thrilling.

Back home, Cate moved around her flat, touching this and that, not able to concentrate on anything specific, just floating along on the memories of the day with Adam. They'd said little to each other, as if words weren't necessary, yet they knew their friendship had deepened and become more significant.

She switched on her computer and brought up her Inbox. There was an e-mail from a customer. Harvey Simpson, who ran a house furnishing company. It was quite up-market and Max had been delighted when they'd secured his business.

She had to read it twice before she understood what Harvey was saying.

*Due to a recent rumour, I am terminating our contract.*

She set off early next morning for Harvey Simpson's showroom. Unfortunately he was away on business and his secretary was reluctant to discuss the matter with her.

'Do you know what this rumour is all about, Maddy?' Cate asked the girl.

'Well, I think he said it was something about non-payment,' she tried not to catch Cate's eye.

'Non-payment of what?' Cate was

confused. Harvey paid her for business services, not the other way about.

Maddy shrugged. 'Rent, or something. For the premises you had with your partner.'

Cate controlled her anger. She couldn't take it out on Maddy. 'That rent was paid in full. I decided to give up the premises when my partner bowed out,' she told her.

'Oh well, maybe Harvey made a mistake,' Maddy looked relieved.

'Who is spreading this rumour?'

'I don't know anything about any rumour.' Maddy's shock was so transparent that Cate knew she was speaking the truth.

'OK.' She smiled at the girl. 'Some confusion here. I'll have a word with Harvey when he returns.'

'He's engaged another company to handle the accounts,' Maddy said in a low whisper.

'Ah,' Cate felt her spirits sink. 'OK, but I still want to speak to him concerning the rumour.'

Cate left Harvey's premises, her mind seething. How and why had this information been revealed now? It had been her major problem when Max walked out. It transpired that he had not paid the rent on their premises for the full year they had occupied them.

That had been one of his responsibilities and he had just ignored it and she had known nothing about it. She had been threatened with court proceedings if she didn't pay the full amount. It had taken all her savings.

Of course, it wouldn't have done the business any good if it had been common knowledge that they'd been defaulting on the rent and she had asked the proprietors of the premises not to make it public knowledge, as a token of good will. Sympathetic to her circumstances, they had promised not to reveal the facts. So who had found out?

She couldn't help a tide of bitterness welling up inside her. Surely after a year Max's betrayal wasn't coming back to haunt her? She felt so angry with herself at the time when she thought back to his lifestyle. Why hadn't she thought twice about the Armani suits, the Gucci watch, the sleek Audi? Had she been so in love that it hadn't occurred to her the money he spent far outweighed the money they earned? She had been so naïve.

By the time she reached the Pagoda Restaurant she had regained her composure. It wouldn't do to be fraught when discussing business with Yee Sung, the restaurant proprietor. He was an extremely gentle and courteous man of some fifty years and entrusted all his paper work to Cate. She admitted it only to herself but he was her favourite client.

He, himself, was in a mood not far short of despairing. It transpired, under Cate's gentle questioning, that he was not serving so many customers these days.

'It's that new place in the mall, Cate,' he explained. 'Everyone is going there to eat Chinese.'

Cate noticed the new Sun Palace, a glitzy place attracting mainly younger customers. 'It is not traditional and soon people will realise that,' she said. 'Your customers have always wanted authentic Chinese food.'

'I wouldn't dream of serving them anything less!' he declared.

'I'll design some new publicity, flyers and a newspaper advertisement.'

'You are clever, Cate, where would I be without you?' Yee Sung joined his hands and bowed.

She hated what she was about to do, but she had resolved that the ugly rumour could have come from one of her customers. She didn't suspect Yee Sung, but he may have heard something himself.

She told him the story and asked if anyone had mentioned it to him. Like Harvey's secretary, the transparent shock on his face told her everything.

'That Max was not a good man. Bad for you. Bad for business.'

Cate could only agree although she

said nothing more to him. She fixed her mind on her plans for his business and left for her flat.

She began a design for the flyer, having taken some copies of Chinese characters from Yee Sung. It was looking good and so when the telephone rang she picked it up eagerly, hoping Adam had spared time to call her.

At first she thought it was a wrong number as no-one spoke, but when she repeated her telephone number, she was aware that there was someone on the other end of the line. There was a long breathy sigh, then the phone was replaced.

She might have dismissed it, if the same thing hadn't happened three more times within the hour. Was it the prankster again . . . but why?

# 4

In some respects working for herself and keeping unsocial hours fitted in rather well with Adam's equally unsocial hours on the police force. Although they talked on the phone every day, they had quickly decided that in order to see each other, they had to take advantage of free time when and where.

So it was that their next meeting fell on Tuesday lunch-time. Cate had the publicity material all ready to show Yee Sung and suggested to Adam that they could lunch at the Pagoda Restaurant.

Cate introduced the two men at the Pagoda, although she made no mention of Adam's profession. She was well aware of Yee Sung assessing him as a suitable escort for her.

Although famous for inscrutability, a quick approving glance at Cate assured her that Adam had passed whatever test

Yee Sung thought appropriate.

'I will study these while you dine.' Yee Sung took Cate's publicity designs and replaced them with the menu.

'I haven't been here before,' Adam said, looking round. 'It has all the atmosphere of a genuine Chinese eating place. Not that I've visited China, but I do read a great deal about other countries and cultures.'

'Do tell Yee Sung,' she said. 'The restaurant isn't doing so well on account of the new place in the mall, hence the reason for the publicity campaign.'

Cate had printed a few copies of the flyer on her computer and she passed one to Adam.

'Where are you going to distribute these?' he asked.

'Public places, anywhere really where potential customers might be.'

'I'll take fifty for the station. I'll make sure every copper has one to take home. I always encourage them to take their wives out on evenings off.' He grinned.

'Adam, that would be fantastic. I suggested new possibilities to Yee Sung in the way of group bookings.'

'More business for him could mean more work for you,' he said. 'Anyway, how is business, you haven't said much on the phone.'

Cate knew she had to choose her words very carefully. One casual reference to any of the happenings of recent days and Adam would pick it up immediately. She had noticed that he listened very carefully to what people said. He wasn't a detective for nothing.

'I'm not at the cutting edge of high-tech business,' she began in a light tone. 'And most people consider accounting and the rest of what I do an excuse to change the subject.'

'You are the subject I'm interested in, so give.' He smiled at her encouragingly.

At that moment the waiter arrived to take their order and Cate had a little more time to think out what to say. She decided to talk about her clients.

'After lunch, I'm off to the Flamingo Sports and Health Centre, do you know it?' she asked.

'The one just off the by-pass?' Adam asked. 'I've been there a couple of times with a mate, although I haven't saved up for membership yet. It's a pretty glitzy place.'

Cate picked up her chopsticks as the chow mein was placed before her. 'It is that — and my best account. It's owned by a really nice couple, Jeff and Laura Dewar. A free swim is one of my perks,' she told him.

'So have you got your cozzy in that briefcase?' he teased.

'It's in the car, actually.'

She had deflected his questions quite neatly she thought as the conversation moved on to sports. They discovered they were both badminton players and decided to set up some games.

'I think I can book a court at the Flamingo for us,' Cate said. 'They do have special rates for non-members.'

'You know, it could be worthwhile our thinking about membership,' Adam said as they tucked into their dessert of lychees.

Cate nodded and smiled. She liked the 'our' in that sentence. It surely meant that Adam felt they would be seeing a lot of each other in future. She forgot all about the hiccups of recent days and focused her thoughts on this new exciting development in her life.

They lingered over green tea until once again Adam's mobile brought their date to an end.

'On the house! On the house!' Yee Sung insisted as they called for the bill. 'Your designs are brilliant, Cate. Please, go ahead and have them printed.'

He helped her on with the cloak and quietly whispered as he did so: 'Good man. Good man for Cate.'

She shook her head slightly at him. It was much too early for that. She had learned to be cautious after her experience with Max.

'We've been in the Pagoda for two hours!' she exclaimed, glancing at her watch when she and Adam left.

'Time flies when you're enjoying yourself.' Adam put his arm round her shoulders, making the old cliché sound much more significant. 'I'll phone you tonight,' he murmured into her hair, after a lingering kiss. 'And if I'm free, can I call round?'

'Anytime,' she told him.

Cate took the newspaper advertisement for the Pagoda to the weekly paper's office, then visited the printer with the flyers and poster to be printed. Then she headed off to the Flamingo Club, humming silly little love songs in her head. She sat in the car park for a few moments when she arrived to compose herself.

Before she went in she rang Harvey Simpson on her mobile. 'The most dreadful thing has happened,' Maddy, his secretary, answered the phone. 'Mr Simpson had a fall in London and he's now in hospital.'

'Oh, I'm so sorry to hear that.' Cate was upset. 'Is he going to be all right?'

'So the doctors say — in the long term — but I reckon he'll be there for a few weeks yet. I don't know when I'll get a chance to talk to him about your account.'

'That's the last thing to worry about,' Cate assured her. 'Please give him my best wishes for a speedy recovery.'

Cate switched off her phone. Her problem was very minor in the grand scale of things. She'd just have to investigate the rumour on her own.

As she made her way into the sports centre, she found that Laura and Jeff were on the point of leaving.

'Hi, Cate, sorry we can't chat. We're off to see a builder,' Laura explained, gathering up keys, handbag and giving last minute instructions to the receptionist.

'We're thinking of expanding, building a bigger gym,' Jeff said. 'We're right in the middle of some tricky negotiations with the guy.'

'We haven't time go over the accounts with you today,' Laura apologised. 'Can you cope on your own? I expect you'll need some extra hours, but you can charge us for those.'

'Sure, no problem,' Cate promised. It was, in fact, a nugget of good news. The extra money would go straight into her savings account. Bit by bit she was trying to build it up to what it had been before Max had left her with the debts. And if Laura and Jeff did expand, their account would expand too!

'I'm off for a swim,' she told them. 'Okay if I leave my briefcase here?'

'Just slide it under the desk,' Jeff said and they left the office.

The swim refreshed her and she was ready for work when she made her way back to the Flamingo office. As usual, Jeff and Laura had left everything in apple pie order and she settled down to give the papers a quick run through in case there were any queries that needed to be sorted out before she took them back to her flat.

One item that she'd had to sell in order to cover the rent debt had been her laptop computer. She missed it dreadfully as it was so invaluable for on the spot work when visiting her clients.

She didn't hear Belinda Clark enter the office, but the overpowering waft of scent told her that the aerobics instructor had arrived.

'It must be wonderful to have a head for figures,' was Belinda's opening shot, delivering in the tone of voice that said only anoraks worked on accounts.

Cate raised her head and summoned a weak smile. Belinda's physical perfection was breath-taking — from her beautifully proportioned figure to her classically oval face with its flawless skin. It was hard not to feel physically inferior.

Cate's figure was trim, her weight correct for her build, her skin was soft and she felt she exuded a sense of good health, but she could never match Belinda's overall impact. So she didn't try. Besides she didn't have cat's claws, she thought as she waited for Belinda's next jibe.

'I suppose that if I'd had the devastating Max Imrie to teach me, then perhaps I might have been tempted to exercise my brain a little more.' This was delivered in a pouting baby voice which grated on Cate.

Belinda somehow managed to look elegant while perching on the end of the desk, smoothing her skin-hugging shocking pink outfit to her body.

'But then, I would have taken such great care not to lose him,' Belinda almost purred the words.

She let a silence hang for a moment, then realising Cate wasn't going to respond, she left the office, pointedly leaving the door open behind her.

Pushing the girl out of her mind, Cate returned to the accounts. It occurred to her that the bad debt rumour could not have reached Laura and Jeff. They would hardly have entrusted her with more business without checking her story. That was one comfort.

She was ready to leave the Flamingo office and go to the bank on her way home when her mobile rang. She grabbed it, hoping it was Adam. But the voice was female and curt.

'Cate. Can you get round her asap.'

'Problem, Erica?' she replied to another of her clients.

'And then some. See you.' The connection was cut.

The bad debt rumour? It was the first thing that jumped into Cate's mind. With mounting trepidation she drove along the by-pass then took a slip road into an older part of Ashrigg. Eventually she bumped along the farm track that led to Erica's pottery. It was housed in an old steading which had been sold off by the farmer. It was ideal for Erica, as she had divided the property into two, the rear part housing her kiln and workshop, while the front was her showroom.

Erica was small and stout, her

overalls matted with clay and paint. Her hair stood up round her head, looking as if it had been clipped with sheep shears.

As usual she didn't bother with a greeting. 'I'm being thrown out!' she almost barked at Cate.

'Of the steading?'

'Yep. Farmer has sold up. New owners want to develop the place for quality housing,' Erica managed a disparaging sneer over the word 'quality'.

'But that's awful. This is a rural area,' Cate said.

'It's also my livelihood!' Erica snapped.

'Yes, of course, I'm sorry,' Cate said at once. 'It's just that your pottery is part of the ambience of the area.'

'Well, you got out of that one neatly,' Erica actually grinned and Cate relaxed a bit.

'So you're on the look-out for new premises,' Cate said.

'That's where you come in,' Erica replied.

The word *premises* had brought back Cate's worry again.

'If you've heard anything . . . ' she began.

'No, I've heard nothing about what's available. You know I'm stuck out here and anyway it's purgatory for me to go into Ashrigg,' Erica replied.

'No, I don't mean that,' Cate plunged in and told her about the rumour.

'Knowing you, it's all been paid now,' Erica said.

'Of course. I stumped up as soon as I got the court order. That situation won't ever happen again to me.'

★ ★ ★

She drove into Ashrigg, collected some brochures for business premises from local estate agents and then made for home. She had a pile of work ahead of her between the Flamingo accounts and studying the brochures. However, if Adam could make it tonight, she'd just put them to one side and get up at dawn to work.

She switched on her computer and

then remembered that she'd meant to go to the bank. Oh well, it was something she would have to do tomorrow.

Soon she was engrossed in the Flamingo accounts and didn't pay much attention when she heard a car stop outside. Then someone put their finger on her door buzzer and just held it there.

Children? Someone in a hurry? She felt inclined to ignore it as she wasn't expecting anyone but the buzz was insistent.

She picked up the entry phone. 'Police!' said a female voice at once. 'Open the door Miss Lindsay. It's D.S. Paterson here. We're coming up.'

She opened the door. D.S. Paterson strode in, accompanied by one of the constables from the previous visit. No Adam. Just the two of them.

'Miss Lindsay,' the sergeant began in a detached tone. 'We would like you to accompany us to the police station. A serious complaint has been made against you.' She stared hard at Cate. 'And this time it is no hoax.'

# 5

Cate stared at D.S. Paterson. She resented the policewoman's attitude. 'Did I hear you correctly? Someone has made a complaint against me?' she asked.

'You did hear me, that's exactly what I said,' Paterson's response verged on the sarcastic. 'One of your clients has made a very serious complaint, which may lead to a charge against you . . . well, almost certainly. This complaint must be dealt with at the police station.'

'Where is Detective Inspector Stone?' Cate asked.

'I've been sent to bring you in,' Paterson was almost smirking.

Sent? By Adam? Why didn't he come? Why didn't he telephone her?

Her mind flashed over the last couple of days. She had done nothing out of the ordinary, taken no decisions on her own apart from Yee Sung's publicity.

'Check her computer,' Paterson turned to the constable.

For a second Cate was paralysed, watching the constable go to her desk and begin sifting through the papers there.

'Just a minute! Don't touch those. Don't touch anything. Those are business papers and private to my clients.' She moved forward to grab the papers.

'We need those for evidence.' Paterson came between her and the desk.

'Evidence of what?' Cate demanded.

'The nature of the complaint that has been made against you.'

'Which is?' Cate forced her voice to remain strong.

'Inspector Stone will inform you. He is interviewing your clients at this moment,' Paterson said.

An icy finger of fear crept up Cate's spine. She didn't like the sound of this at all. Adam interviewing her clients?

Could this have anything to do with the bad debt rumour?

The constable was leafing through her papers.

'I asked you to leave those,' she said icily. 'I have three client accounts there. What you are doing amounts to an invasion of privacy.'

'I have to do my job,' the constable said, not unkindly. 'Some of these could refer to the client concerned.'

'I have to protect every client's privacy,' she told him.

'That's one way of disguising you have something to hide,' Paterson commented.

Cate could see there was no profit in continuing this conversation. Paterson was against her and, come to think of it, had been, over the kidnap hoax. Perhaps it was her police training but she thought it was more of an attitude. Something to do with Adam? Quite possibly. Anyway, the sooner this was sorted out the better.

'Take what you have to, but I will be

consulting my lawyer about this,' Cate informed them. 'Now, let's get it all sorted out.' She marched out of the room into the bedroom and returned wearing her red cloak.

At the station, she did not have the same ordeal of handing over her handbag, but instead was shown straight into an ordinary room. She was left alone and noted with some relief that this did not appear to be an interview room and there were no tapes set up.

It was a good fifteen minutes later before Adam appeared with the sergeant. During that time she had tried hard not to think why Adam hadn't phoned her to say a complaint had been made. Why had he let Paterson come to the flat without any warning?

Whatever his reasons. She was no wiser when he entered the room. He didn't speak, only gave her an unsmiling nod and took a chair near the window.

Cate was appalled. Was this the same man with whom she'd shared so many happy hours, in whose arms she'd nestled, comforted and thrilled by his kisses?

As if on cue, Paterson sat down opposite her and said: 'Same red cloak, Miss Lindsay. I thought you would have gone off it.'

Cate didn't think that was worth a reply.

Paterson opened a buff-coloured file which she'd brought into the room with her and said: 'Right now.'

Why was Adam taking no part in this? Cate forced herself to keep from looking at him. Did his silent presence mean he suspected her of something?

'We have received a complaint from one of your clients that you have misappropriated funds from their accounts,' the sergeant said.

Cate forgot Adam! Misappropriation of funds! That was an accountant's nightmare. She thought of all the accounts she dealt with this week. She hadn't got as far as utilising any client's funds. She hadn't even made it to the bank.

She found her voice. 'There must be some mistake. I have not touched any funds in the last week.'

'We have evidence to the contrary,' the sergeant said.

'Evidence?' Cate's voice wavered. Not again. For a moment she felt she had fallen into a time slip. The conversation was almost identical to the one she'd had with Adam over the false kidnap.

Paterson rustled the papers in the file. 'Today you authorised your bank to transfer £10,000 from the account of the Flamingo Sports Club to your business account.'

'I did no such thing!' Cate was taken completely by surprise. 'I was at the Sports Club only today . . . '

'You agree that you have access to their account and authority to draw money on it?'

'Yes,' she replied to the sergeant. 'But I didn't make any transfers today.'

'The facts state differently,' Paterson replied.

'What facts?' Cate's initial shock was being transmuted into anger. She determined that there would be no repeat of the false accusations of last time.

'I have here a bank transfer slip, signed by you, authorising the transfer of the money stated from the Flamingo account into the account of Enterprise Expertise. That is the name of your business, is it not?' Paterson held the piece of paper by her fingertips.

'May I see it?' Cate stretched her hand across the table.

It was passed over and she studied it. It was just as Paterson had said. All the details were correct — the account numbers of both the Flamingo and her business. Today's date. The signature at the bottom of the slip was hers. But she hadn't signed it.

'Inspector Stone was contacted by Mr and Mrs Dewar after their lawyer had been in touch with the bank and discovered the transfer,' the sergeant told her.

That was another shock. Jeff and Laura had contacted the police before speaking to her? How could they have done that? She'd given them nothing but loyal service.

'I did not make this transaction. I was not even in the bank today. My business is entirely trustworthy. As you may remember from my last visit here, I do not take anything that does not belong to me,' she couldn't help adding.

Paterson picked up on that immediately. 'Perhaps you made that kidnap hoax call yourself to gain sympathy and so deflect us from suspecting you in this case.'

Before she could reply, Adam barked: 'Paterson!'

The girl flushed dark red. 'I withdraw that.'

Cate said nothing. Did not even look at Adam. Could not look at him. He must suspect her of this theft if he'd taken the trouble to interview Jeff and Laura. And what of them? Did they really think she would be stupid enough to steal from them?

She felt like crushing the bank slip in her fingers, but instead took another look at the details. It was an excellent forgery of her signature. She hid a sigh. All her clients were familiar with her signature, so how on earth was she going to prove her innocence?

Then a thought struck her. 'What evidence do you have that I personally paid this into the bank since it wasn't an electronic transaction?' she asked the sergeant.

'The bank teller remembers you. His name is Rankine.' The sergeant held out her hand for the bank slip.

Cate held on to it. 'I don't know him. How can he be sure that I was the person who made the transaction?'

'Oh he was quite definite. He said the woman who gave him the instructions was wearing a red cloak . . . quite distinctive . . . with green trimming.' Paterson paused. 'And you told us yourself, Miss Lindsay, your cloak is unique, not another one in Ashrigg or anywhere else for that matter.'

Cate felt herself ready to slump in the chair and resigned herself to handing over the slip, when a detail caught her eye.

'The time of the transaction is stated as 1.30 p.m.' she said.

'That's correct,' Paterson said. 'Mr Rankine had just returned from his lunch break.'

Cate let out a relieved sigh. 'And if I can prove that I couldn't possibly have been at the bank at that time, what then?'

Paterson took the slip of paper from Cate's hands, but didn't lose eye contact. 'We would need a witness as to your whereabouts at that time.'

'I was having lunch in the Pagoda Restaurant,' she told her.

Paterson allowed a small smile to play around her lips. 'Ah, but that is owned by Yee Sung . . . one of your clients, I believe?'

'He will confirm I was there,' Cate said evenly.

'Not good enough. He could be a favourable witness. You will have to come up with something better, Miss Lindsay.'

Cate sat and let the silence stretch out.

Then Adam spoke. 'Miss Lindsay was with me at the Pagoda Restaurant from one o'clock until three. She was not out of my sight for two hours. You should have presented the bank slip to me before bringing Miss Lindsay to the station, Sergeant Paterson.'

Fifteen minutes later Cate was free to go. Paterson said she would check with Mr Rankine again about the description of the person who'd made the transaction and that the bank's video film would be examined.

Cate insisted that the bank be told to transfer the money back to the Flamingo without delay and that the Dewars should be informed that it had been a fraudulent transaction by a person unknown.

'There are a number of issues to be

addressed here,' Adam spoke to her for the first time and she could hear the note of apology in his tone.

She ignored it. 'Yes, indeed,' she replied without looking at him. 'Such as who forged my signature and once again impersonated me. But I shall attend to those on my own. I obviously cannot rely on the police force to support me.'

'Cate!' Adam reached out for her, oblivious of Paterson watching them.

But she rushed from the room and out of the station before he could stop her. All her dreams of being with Adam lay in ruins. The very basis of a loving relationship had been shown to be non-existent. He couldn't trust her.

She found a taxi, got home, threw herself into the house, stumbled upstairs to her flat. She was too shocked and sick at heart to do any work at all. She knew she should telephone the Dewars, but was still hurt by the fact they hadn't bothered to check with her before involving the police.

She sat on her sofa, staring at nothing, unaware of the shadows lengthening in the room. When the phone rang she almost jumped out of her skin, but then cold reason asserted itself and she guessed it would be Adam. She picked up the receiver and dumped it in the waste paper basket before leaving the living-room and closing the door firmly behind her.

She woke the next morning after a turbulent night. But she woke in a spirit of determination and resolve. She had to take charge of her life and her business. Someone out there was causing mischief and she'd been too naïve to see what was happening.

She would not endure a re-run of the situation that she had suffered when Max left. Then she'd been crushed by his abandonment of her and the business and it had taken a long time for her self-esteem to return.

Now she knew she was on her own

again. But she was a responsible, conscientious accountant. No-one could throw mud at her, or if they did, they would find out that it didn't stick.

First thing she rang the Flamingo, but the receptionist told her that Jeff and Laura were not available. Cate didn't believe her, but knew she was probably acting on orders. A face-to-face confrontation was therefore necessary.

She decided not to rush out, but leave it until later when perhaps the Dewars wouldn't be expecting her.

She switched on her answering machine before she left the flat. It would stay on for as long as necessary. She'd let it take all the calls and then she'd decide if she wanted to return any. That way she could avoid speaking to Adam and also frustrate whoever had made the silent calls earlier.

This morning she planned to visit another client, Paola Trevi who ran the Café Felice with typical Italian flair. There were always subtle aromas of garlic competing with coffee, giving an authentic Mediterranean atmosphere to the establishment.

'Ciao!' Paola greeted Cate when she arrived and immediately instructed her assistant to fetch coffee.

Paola wasn't a hands-on owner, as Cate had noticed before, but left most of the work to her assistant and the two teenage girls who served the tables.

'Great, I need to relax,' Cate said. And this was the place to do it. No pressure here. Paola had approached her soon after arriving in Ashrigg and opened the café less than a year ago. She was Cate's very own client, not someone who'd been with the business when Max was around. And, as such, Paola would know nothing about his defection or indeed the bad debt rumour.

'How's business?' Cate asked automatically as Paola brought the coffee and pastry and took the seat opposite her at the table.

'Is good,' Paola replied. 'No, is much better. Many people are coming to the mall and they all want to eat and drink!' she gave a chuckle.

Cate suspected that Paola herself was part of the attraction at the café. She was a pretty woman with dark luxuriant hair which cascaded down her back. Her accent was beguiling with its broken English, but with occasional echoes of another, less warm tongue. Cate thought she could probably speak several languages.

'I have some new suppliers. I will give you all my paperwork. Remember now, Cate, you must work miracles with the tax man!' Paola smiled, opening her eyes widely, highlighting the deep brown irises.

'I wish I could! My best is all I can promise.'

Relaxed and cheered by the interlude in the café, Cate soon set off for the sports club. Entering by a back door, she bypassed the receptionist and went straight to their office. Jeff and Laura looked most uncomfortable when she breezed in.

'Why didn't you speak to me first?' Cate asked, determined to cut through any waffle.

'We went to the builder, got a price, then carried on to our lawyer,' Jeff explained hurriedly. 'While we were there, he decided to call the bank, just to check on a possible loan. He was told about the £10,000 being transferred from our account to yours.'

'Our lawyer insisted that we went directly to the police,' Laura added. 'He said it was the only way to handle it.'

'We met Detective Inspector Stone at the front desk and we told him about the theft right away,' Jeff continued.

'Did you really think I'd steal from you?' Cate asked.

There was a short silence and the couple exchanged a glance. 'We have always trusted you, Cate, but we heard . . . ' Jeff stopped and looked out of the window.

'Heard what?' Cate asked, although she guessed what was coming.

'That you had a bad debt, rent unpaid.'

'That's absolutely true,' Cate watched their astonished expressions.

'But that all happened a year ago. My former partner, Max, had omitted to pay rent on our premises and I knew nothing about it until he'd gone. I paid up immediately. If you care to check with the rental company concerned I have their telephone number here.'

Both looked even more embarrassed.

'Who told you about that debt?' Cate asked.

Again they exchanged a glance. 'No-one actually spoke to us. A note was left at reception,' Laura said.

'Anonymous?' Cate asked, although she already knew the answer.

Jeff nodded.

'Do you still have it?'

'No. It came about a week ago. And we don't have time for people who send anonymous notes. We chucked it out and we did mean to mention it to you yesterday, but we forgot in the rush to meet the builder,' Laura said apologetically.

'But you did believe it in the end,' Cate said.

'What were we to think when we heard about the bank transfer?' Jeff asked.

Cate sighed.

'There's also the question of your security,' he continued.

'My security?' Cate was puzzled.

'The police have told us that someone impersonated you and forged your signature accurately.'

'Yes, that's right,' Cate agreed.

'Surely all the work you do for your clients should be kept private. Someone clearly had access to your signature, your bank account number and ours, so it was easy to make a fraudulent transaction,' Jeff said.

'All my clients are familiar with my signature, even you. I was not in the bank yesterday and I have police proof of that. Nevertheless I'm also investigating this whole thing on my own and I can assure you it won't happen again,' she said.

'Cate . . . we can't take a chance, can't afford anything to go wrong with our new extension plans,' Laura said.

'I understand that but what are you getting at?' Cate asked.

'We feel we have no option but to terminate our contract with you and employ a new accountant,' Jeff said.

# 6

Cate decided to have her usual swim before leaving the Flamingo. She knew it would relieve the tension in her body and besides the Dewars were insistent that she make use of all the facilities there, free of charge. She guessed they were feeling guilty at their summary dismissal of her, as they had been friends, but as she knew only too well, business was business.

The bottom line, of course, was the fact that this anonymous person had lost her two accounts now. First Harvey Simpson's and now the Flamingo. She simply had to find out who was at the back of it.

She was walking down the corridor towards the exit after her swim when Belinda sashayed out from the gym.

'So it's goodbye then, Cate, dear,' Belinda gave a theatrical sigh.

'Word gets around fast,' Cate said, not stopping in her stride, but disappointed that the Dewars had told Belinda.

'It was such a drama yesterday,' she went on, matching Cate's steps.

Cate pushed open the door and let it swing back, but Belinda caught it. 'Well, a big security lapse here would be, wouldn't it?' Cate threw the words over her shoulder.

'What security lapse?' Belinda's tone sharpened.

'Its possible that my briefcase was searched. I left it in the Dewars' office while I was in the pool. Everyone who has access to the office must be checked. Someone got hold of the Dewars' account number.'

Cate unlocked her car door and slipped into the driving seat. She closed the door and wound down the driver window.

She looked up at Belinda and gave her a false smile. 'You will tell the police everything, won't you?' she asked.

'The police?' Belinda's voice rose an octave.

'Mmm, they'll be round to interview everyone who was here at the same time as me yesterday. Of course, the only person I remember seeing in the office was you.' She switched on the engine.

'But I didn't . . . ' Belinda began.

As she drove on to the road Cate reflected that was a cheap shot, especially as she didn't think Belinda had anything to do with invading her security. She didn't think the girl would have had the nerve or guile to do that. Belinda was all appearance.

She was also a gossip and that was where Cate's words would do most good. Belinda would be sure to spread it around the Flamingo that the police intended to question staff and members. Actually, Cate had no idea if Adam and his cohorts would investigate at the Sports Centre, but the bald fact was that she was now not taking any prisoners. She was fighting for her livelihood.

Despite her swim she could still feel the tension in her shoulders. She didn't want to go back to the flat. She'd collect all the Flamingo papers and return them tomorrow. Otherwise, her client base was up to date.

Despite the loss of the two major contracts, she still had a sound complement of clients. Many of them were self-employed, such as tradesmen, or writers, and others who worked from home. For those, she mainly handled their tax returns and any other small details.

However, it wouldn't do any harm to sound out new business prospects. It might be a good idea to cast her net farther afield. She thought of her mother and her antique shop in Stirling. Maybe some of her associates could do with an accountant? Worth a try.

Without another thought she took the main road for Stirling.

'Dear girl,' her father greeted her

with a kiss. 'Your mother is away at an auction today and I'm minding the store.'

'That's very noble of you,' she teased. 'There must be desolation over all Scotland's golf courses.'

'Probably there is!' he retorted, smoothing back his silver grey hair with all the manner of a matinee idol.

Cate hadn't failed to notice that he was actually, apart from the shoes, dressed in golfing gear. 'You're expecting her back in time for you to play a few holes, not just the nineteenth?' she asked.

'Hope springs eternal, but you know that once your mother gets into an auction room, it's like trying to get a winkle out of a shell to remove her.'

'I'll take over until she gets back, if you like,' Cate offered.

Her father studied her. 'On the one hand, I think you need a break from your job. I don't like the look of those dark circles under your eyes. On the other hand, if you do nothing, you'll just worry at whatever problem you have.'

Cate smiled at him. Perhaps he saw more than she suspected, understood more about her struggle since Max went. 'There's a little method in my madness,' she confessed. 'I have a notion to take on more clients and thought I might spread my talents to some of Mum's customers.'

'Good thinking. Many of them have more money than sense, paying some of her prices,' he laughed. 'I'll keep my mobile switched on in case you need a hand.'

Cate reflected that being in the shop was just the tonic she needed. She loved the old furniture, the porcelain and, most of all, the paintings. She felt a brief echo of pain when she thought of Adam and how he'd be interested in seeing some of the paintings, but she firmly banished him from her thoughts.

She set out a pile of her business cards, ready to hand to every customer who came in regardless of whether they needed an accountant or not. After all, they would have family, friends, etc. She smiled to herself. She was becoming very assertive. Just as she should have been when Max was around.

★  ★  ★

Adam had given up ringing Cate's home number. It was the answering machine every time. He didn't try her mobile. He wanted no distractions when he spoke to her and he guessed she might be involved with clients.

Every time he'd driven close to Croft Road, he'd called in and pressed her buzzer. No reply. He wondered if she'd gone to stay with family.

He'd had a word with his Chief Inspector, advising him that he knew Cate personally and it had been decided that the investigation into the Flamingo fraud attempt should be handled by Sergeant Paterson.

Adam had agreed reluctantly as his sergeant was hardly sympathetic to

Cate. Julie Paterson had been a good choice for his detective sergeant when she arrived at Ashrigg. He'd given her as much training as possible and she had shaped up very well. His one mistake had been to take her out for dinner one evening at the conclusion of a successful case.

Julie had completely misread the invitation, taking it for something more personal. Although he had never repeated it, he knew she was still hopeful that he was interested in her. Somehow she had sensed his attraction to Cate and he guessed that an element of jealousy was at the root of her attitude.

He'd had a tactful word with her that morning, not mentioning Cate's name, but explaining that her interviewing methods would not lead to early promotion. It was a kind of double-edged comment. They both knew that promotion would mean her leaving Ashrigg. It was as big a hint as he could give that they had no future together.

Since the previous evening, he'd spent long hours at his computer, checking out everything he could about Cate. Not only her business clients, but also whatever personal details he could find. There wasn't much left of anyone's life that couldn't be learned with access to the right data.

Sergeant Paterson was examining the bank video in detail. He'd watched it himself and could see no way that the impersonator could easily be identified. The red cloak was prominent, but she had also worn a scarf on her head and kept her back to the video camera at all times. This was either luck on her part, or she was a professional thief.

Adam now drove out to Heronsfield to see if he could locate Cate. She had been open with him about her sister and lawyer husband and it had been easy to access their address.

He drove past slowly, noting the absence of Cate's car. A Fiesta was parked in the drive. Probably her sister's. He moved off. He could hardly barge in and ask if she knew where Cate was.

Finding her mother's antique shop was relatively easy too. Adam parked across the road and thought out his next move. He would go in and have a look at some paintings, possibly even buy one if it was in his price range and then let general talk drift on to family and friends. He'd casually mention he came from Ashrigg and a pound to a penny her mother would say she had a daughter who lived there.

He found in his job that people were usually very happy to talk about their children and he guessed Cate's mother would be as friendly and open as she was.

It might be a little underhand to work in this way, but then he desperately needed to see Cate. He was now convinced that she was being deliberately stalked by someone. Who knew what it might escalate to?

He left his car and crossed the road.

The shop had once been a cottage and the lower windows were bay, with some panes of bottle glass. He took a moment or two to examine the display in the windows and then peered into the shop to see if it was busy.

He looked straight into Cate's eyes. Quickly he moved to the door, but not before she dropped the sneck and switched the Open/Closed sign to the latter.

He knocked on the door. 'Cate, let me in. It's vital that we talk!'

Through the glass panel he could see her retreating into the back shop. He stood for a moment, wondering whether to locate the back door of the premises or return to the car and wait until she finally came out.

'What's all this?'

He spun round at the sound of the outraged voice and came face to face with an elegant lady, dressed in plum-coloured skirt and shawl. Pewter hair framed a face that still held elements of Cate's own features, but her eyes were lighter than her daughter's even though they were now sparkling with energy.

'The shop appears to be closed,' Adam said.

'Nonsense, it's only the middle of the afternoon. If my husband has skived off to the golf course . . . ' she hammered on the door. 'Malcolm!'

Adam waited in silence and eventually saw Cate reappear in the shop. She crossed to the door and undid the lock.

'Cate, darling, how lovely to see you.' Her mother moved into the shop, only stopping to switch the sign back to *Open*. As she did so, Adam saw his chance and slipped in behind her.

'This gentleman was waiting to come in. Did you and Dad forget to open up after lunch?'

Cate murmured a reply and Adam seized the opportunity.

'Hi, Cate, for a moment I thought I'd missed you,' he said easily.

'Oh, my goodness, I didn't know you

were my daughter's friend,' her mother said.

'Mother, this is Adam Stone. Mr Stone, my mother Mrs Lindsay,' Cate was forced to make the introductions, but didn't look once at Adam. 'I came by and offered to look after the shop while Dad went off to the golf course.'

'That was kind of you, my dear. Have you had a busy day?' Mrs Lindsay asked, but her eyes were darting back and forward between Adam and Cate.

'Yes, quite a few sales,' Cate's voice was almost toneless.

'Good girl, well I can take over now,' Mrs Lindsay said archly.

'Then maybe we can set off on our date,' Adam smoothly suggested to Cate. He was rewarded with a glare. 'Or do you want to stay and talk over things here?'

He knew at once that she saw where that was heading. He suspected that she'd told her parents nothing about the impersonator.

Once outside and out of view from

the shop, Cate turned to him. 'We have nothing to talk about. I'm going home,' she said through gritted teeth.

'We have a great deal to talk about Cate. For one thing we have to sort out this problem with your impersonator. That was a very serious incident yesterday. It must never happen again. Now, get in my car and we'll go to Owlsmoor where we can talk with no interruptions from outside.'

Cate turned to him, indecision clouding her eyes. 'Please!' he opened the passenger door of his car.

Reluctantly, she stepped inside where she sat hunched, silent, for the first couple of miles. Adam said nothing too. He wanted to wait until they were in the isolated cottage where he could speak to her quietly and without argument.

'I thought you said we were going to Owlsmoor. This is not the way,' she said eventually, sitting up and taking notice.

'I'm taking a roundabout route for security reasons.' It was a bit strong, but he sensed he was going to have to emphasise or even exaggerate a little to make Cate understand the seriousness of the situation.

Once inside the cottage, he lit the fire and then briskly made some coffee. Cate had curled up in an armchair.

He handed her a mug and then drew up a footstool in front of her chair. 'The most important reason we've come here is because I want to tell you that I care for you more than anyone I've ever cared for,' he said, looking straight into her eyes.

The words didn't go halfway to conveying that he really loved her. She wasn't ready for that yet and he knew she'd been deeply hurt by his silence at the station the day before.

She made no comment nor did her expression change.

'If I had my way, I'd keep you here, safe and warm, forever.' He paused. 'I know you thought I had betrayed you yesterday and believe me it devastated me too.'

He watched as she took a sip of coffee. 'Just like you I have a job to do,' he went on. 'Just like you there are rules that I must follow. I was powerless to interfere yesterday as the situation had developed in a way that I couldn't change.'

Her eyes flickered briefly in his direction. 'The Dewars came charging into the station demanding attention. I happened to be at the front desk and due to the seriousness of their complaint had to attend to them straight away. I had no chance to leave them and telephone you,' he explained. 'Paterson thought she was doing the right thing by bringing you in, although she omitted to check with me.'

Cate drained her coffee mug and reached out to put it on the table.

Adam took the opportunity to take hold of her hand. She didn't pull away. 'My officers are dealing with this fraud, but my concern is protecting you, Cate. You have to believe me,' he appealed to her.

'Nobody is going to con me again,' she said quietly.

'I'm not conning you about my feelings,' he said quietly.

'I want to believe you, Adam, but my life seems to be falling apart.'

'I went to the Flamingo today and learned you'd lost their account,' he said. 'That is all due to your impersonator.'

'Well, perhaps not entirely. It's due to a bad debt rumour about me which is untrue.'

'Surely they didn't cancel your contract on account of a rumour?' he asked.

'Another client did.'

'When did that happen?'

'Last week.'

'Why didn't you tell me?'

'Well, it's hardly a police matter.'

'Maybe not then, but now it looks more serious. Besides, I thought we were close, telling each other everything. How did this rumour come about?'

'My ex-partner Max left the business without warning and I only discovered later that he hadn't paid the rent on our premises for the whole year we'd been there.'

'Did you have to pay it?'

'I settled it immediately. And when I first heard the rumour I checked with the rental company. They'd kept it confidential since I'd paid.'

'I wonder if your impersonator and the rumour could be linked. Two clients have been told about the rumour. And she's impersonated you twice.'

'Three times.'

'Cate, for Pete's sake! What else haven't you been telling me?'

'My car wouldn't start,' she paused. 'My brother-in-law Rob checked it over when he ran me back home next day. A wire had been disconnected.'

'I don't believe this! Why didn't you tell me!' he exploded.

'What was there to tell?' Cate was roused to anger. 'It's hardly a crime to dress identically and anyone could have fiddled with the car. I have no proof.'

Adam ran his fingers through his hair. 'Right. This has gone far enough. The whole thing has to be thoroughly investigated. I can't deal with it officially as I've told my Chief Inspector we have a personal connection,' he said. 'But I'm determined to get to the bottom of this.'

He leaned towards her. 'First of all, tell me all about Max.'

# 7

'Max?' Cate was surprised. 'He's been away for a year. Why do you ask?'

'I had to check your business background when the problem with the Dewars arose. I found that you and Max Imrie had been joint directors of Enterprise Expertise. What exactly happened?'

Cate held her hands towards the fire as if hoping to gain some warmth before telling Adam the cold facts. 'As I said already he upped and left one day, without warning. Just an e-mail on my laptop to say that he'd had a better offer from Sydney.'

'So you took over the business and the debts?'

'Yes. When we set up we divided the work so that I dealt with all the incoming cash and he paid the bills. Or so I thought.'

'He didn't steal from your clients?'

'No, fortunately. It was the first thing I checked after I got the rent summons.' She twisted her hands and looked directly at Adam for the first time. 'I was ignorant — no, naïve, is probably the better word for it. I was so thrilled to be running a business, that I put compete trust in his hands.'

'And he abused it. What would have happened if you hadn't been able to pay up?' he asked.

She shrugged. 'I would have lost everything.'

'Would he have known that?'

She didn't answer for a moment. 'I rather doubt he cared. But I was determined to carry on, using every last cent of my savings. That was the one part of my dignity that I held on to.'

'Did you care for him?'

She again looked him in the eye. 'At the time, yes. And I was completely fooled. I just accepted that he was able to swan around in Armani suits, Gucci shoes, have the latest sports car, take me for gourmet meals. Can you imagine that I was so blinkered that I didn't really ask where the money was coming from?'

'It was coming from your business,' Adam nodded.

'Exactly. I was paying for those, if you like, or rather I did pay for them in the end. It was a hard lesson, but I learned a lot about myself.'

Adam lifted her up from the chair and held her hands in his. 'I know it must have looked as if I didn't trust you at the station yesterday . . . ' he began.

She nodded, a weariness making her shoulders droop. 'I know, you've explained your reasons, but you can't blame me for being a little shell-shocked.' She let go of his hands and wandered over to the window.

Adam came up behind her but didn't touch her.

'The sun is about to disappear — can that be said too of our misunderstanding? Could we make a fresh start tomorrow — a new day?'

She turned to look at him. He knew

she saw the longing in his eyes, he waited for a sign from her. It was the briefest of nods, but it held a kernel of hope. He decided not to press the emotional charge any farther.

'Let's sit down and work on a strategy for sorting out these problems.' Gently he led her back to the sofa. 'The first thing is your cloak. I want you to put it into the dry cleaners — and keep the ticket in a safe place. Then if you are impersonated again, you have proof you couldn't possibly be guilty of whatever crime she has set up.'

'Mmm, I take your point, but she knows my car registration, where I live.'

'There are ways round that. Taxis. Living here,' he said.

She stared at him. 'Here at Owlsmoor? But this is your secret place.'

'I'd like it to be yours, too.'

She gazed at him for a long moment. He knew she'd understand he was offering more than a safe hideaway.

'I don't know . . . it sounds as if I'm running away from all my problems.'

'It's only until we sort out who's behind the impersonation and the rumour. It could well be the same person,' he told her.

'Yes, I've been wondering about that. But I want to take her on, Adam.'

'Sure, I understand. I think the first thing is to find out which accountancy firm Harvey Simpson and the Dewars have registered with. It could be someone touting for business and doing it in an underhand way.'

'I never thought of that.' For the first time she smiled. 'Of course, you're the detective.' She stood up and picked up her cloak.

'Thanks for everything, Adam. You've made me look at things in a different way. I really need to go home now and think.'

He didn't stop her. He sensed she needed some time alone.

'I'll drive you back to Stirling and you can collect your car. But remember the first thing you do in the morning is put that cloak into the dry cleaners.'

★ ★ ★

Back home, Cate placed the keys to Owlsmoor on her bedside table. She was too mixed up to think if she would ever use them. It would take her some time to sort out her feelings for Adam.

There was no doubt that he was completely genuine about solving her problems. They'd agreed she would find out which accountancy firms had taken on the accounts of Harvey Simpson and the Flamingo.

Adam, meanwhile, would go to the sports centre, unofficially, and try to establish who might have had access to her briefcase while she had been swimming. She'd told him about Belinda, but also her belief that the girl was not capable of any underhand activity.

'You thought that about Max Imrie, didn't you?' he said. 'You are by nature a trusting person. I am, by training, a suspicious devil.'

She managed to raise a smile.

'With your permission I'll interview your other clients, but again not wearing my policeman's hat. And don't worry, they won't realise they are being interrogated. I'll be the perfect under-cover man.'

She had to admit she was glad of his help and he'd given her some tips on how to handle things.

So, first thing next day she tele-phoned the Dewars at the Flamingo and said she would hand over all their financial papers to their new accoun-tant personally and asked for his name.

Adam had told her that if she went in person to the sports club, they might just take the papers without revealing the name of her successor.

'Oh,' Laura was obviously taken by surprise. 'Our lawyer suggested a company in Edinburgh. He said it was highly respectable, so we thought it would be tightly run.' She gave a little gasp. 'Sorry, I didn't mean it to come out that way, Cate, but there's just such a big investment at stake here.'

'I understand,' Cate said, keeping her tone even.

'Our lawyer said he would take our papers and pass them on.'

'Fine. Just for my records, can I have the name of the accountancy firm? After what happened yesterday, I am not prepared to hand over anything until I know exactly where it is going.'

'Yes, of course,' Laura said in a rush and told her the name. 'I hope we see you here at the centre soon. We certainly don't want to lose touch.'

'No fear of that,' Cate said briskly. 'I might even become a member.' She was not going to let anyone think she was crawling away to lick her wounds.

Besides, Adam had suggested at one time that they should both join the sports club. Well, that issue was on the back burner for the meantime.

Next Cate went once again to Harvey Simpson's office. She reckoned that his secretary, Maddy, was sympathetic towards her and anyway she had to hand over his files.

Maddy was open with her information but it was disquieting to find that Harvey's business was now with the same accounting firm in Edinburgh as the Dewars. Was it just coincidence? Maybe she could get Adam to make a few enquiries.

Her next visit was to Erica's pottery with the brochures she'd collected for possible new premises.

'About time,' Erica grumbled. 'Do you realise how long it will take me to set up my kiln and all the other necessities in a new location? I need to move fast.'

'What you need is an already vacant property.'

'Well done, Sherlock Holmes,' Erica said without rancour.

'So, all the properties in these brochures are either empty or up for a quick sale,' Cate said, trying to conceal her triumph.

'Huh. Well, hang around and we'll go and check out some. First, there is a customer standing behind you.'

'Oh, sorry,' Cate turned round and looked straight into Adam's eyes. She caught the warning look.

'Can I help?' Erica wiped her hands on her dungarees.

'Hope so. Looking for soup bowls,' Adam said.

Cate drifted off to stand near Erica's workshop, trying not to catch his eye.

Erica showed him a selection. 'Nice lay-out you have here. I couldn't help overhearing you were thinking of moving,' he said casually.

'No choice. Compulsory purchase.'

'Life's tough, especially when you're on your own,' he said.

After he bought a set of soup bowls, he strolled to the door, pausing to let Cate pass by on her way to her car. She'd told Erica she'd wait outside for her.

'Wrong height to impersonate you,' Adam said quietly as they walked towards their cars. 'And no-one else working for her.'

Cate's stomach flipped. That was something she'd never thought of.

But, no, not Erica. For one thing she cared little for the world outside her pottery. And secondly, she was so straightforward, she'd have nothing to do with anything underhand.

'Have you put your cloak into the cleaners yet?' he murmured as Erica locked her barn door.

'On my way now,' she said.

'Can I meet you in Stirling? I'd like to have a look at some of the paintings your mother is selling.'

★ ★ ★

Adam had taken two days' leave to enable him to check out Cate's clients. As he feared Sergeant Paterson had reached stalemate with identifying the bank fraud impersonator. Not that it was her fault, there was just nothing to go on. She'd interviewed Jeff and Laura and asked them about office security, which they admitted was not perfect, but that they trusted all their employees.

She had gained access to the log

book and made note of the times their instructors had booked in and out. Adam had read this and taken note. Cate had mentioned Belinda, so he decided he would chat her up.

There was no sign of the Dewars when he pitched up at reception, so he had no problems about explaining his unofficial presence. He asked if he could look around with the intention of becoming a member.

It didn't take him long to find Belinda Clark. Cate had given him a full description and he spotted her coming out of the gym.

'Excuse me,' he said. 'I'm just having a nosey here, might join in fact. The thing is, I need a strong coffee at the moment. Could you direct me to the café?'

She wagged a long finger at him. 'People don't come here to drink coffee for their health!' She gave him a 1,000 watt smile.

'Well, maybe you can cure me,' he flirted a little.

'You need a smoothie, I think.' She gave his body a once-over assessment. 'Come on, I'll take you there and show you what your body craves.'

She chatted vacuously all the way to the café. 'Bit of a stramash here yesterday, I gather,' he said as they sat down at a table with a mango smoothie each. To ease his conscience he had paid for hers.

Belinda's eyes widened dramatically, but mainly for effect on him. 'Oh, you've heard! Mind you, the accountant had it coming to her. She was so lax with security. I'm so surprised she was able to run that business at all.'

'Why is that?' he asked, keeping up the gossipy tone.

'Her partner ditched her and if you ask me he was the clever one. He had style, class.'

'What happened to him?'

'Well,' Belinda paused again for maximum effect. 'She, that Cate Lindsay, said he went to Sydney to a better job.'

'And did he?'

'That is the 64 million dollar question, so to speak. Nobody has ever heard from him. He left without warning, without telling any of his clients — just ask the Dewars. Or, for that matter, without telling his friends.' There was a suggestion of a pout. 'I think it's time someone found out exactly what happened to Max Imrie.'

\* \* \*

Cate was about to head off for Stirling when she took a call on her mobile. It was Paola Trevi from the Café Felice.

'Cate, my staff want an increase in their wages. Can you call and see me pronto? Ciao.'

She sent Adam a text. At Café Felice with client Paola Trevi. Be with you asap. If at antique shop say nothing about my problems.

'Ah, Cate,' Paola greeted her effusively. 'My staff keep wanting more and more money. Can I afford this?'

Cate knew Paola paid them the minimum wage, but also that working in the café was really hard work. They probably deserved a rise. She took from her briefcase a summary of Paola's income and expenditure.

'Give me a minute to work out something,' she said, busy with her calculator. A few minutes later she put the figures before Paola. 'I think that's an acceptable wage rise for them.'

Paola shrugged. 'Business had better improve.' Nevertheless she ordered a cappuccino and croissant with jam for Cate.

She was just finishing her coffee when the café door swung open and to her surprise Yee Sung appeared. He looked extremely distressed. He had one of Cate's flyers in his hand.

'She is here now,' Paola said to him. 'I met Yee Sung in the mall and I told him you were coming to see me.'

'Cate, what has happened?' he began. 'There has been a terrible mistake,' the hand holding the flyer shook.

Cate jumped up. 'What is it?'

'A disaster,' Paola said. 'It is the flyers and poster you designed for him.'

Cate took a flyer from Yee Sung's hands. At first it seemed exactly as she had given it to the printer, then Yee Sung pointed to the bottom.

The address for the Pagoda Restaurant was wrong. It was in fact, the address of the brash new Chinese restaurant in the mall. Yee Sung's rival.

'How on earth did that happen?'

'When I collected these the printer said you had made the alterations.' Yee Sung's voice trembled.

'What? The address is wrong. Why would I do that?' was Cate's first reaction.

Yee Sung shrugged. 'I don't understand. He said you authorised the change and he has already distributed some in Ashrigg.'

'Caterina, are you all right?' Paola asked, as Cate sat down in her chair again.

'I did not make this change,' Cate

told Yee Sung. 'I have not been near the printer since I left the original flyer with him — and it was correct.'

'What am I to do? I will have no customers now and have lost all that money in the printing.' He raised his eyes to her. 'The printer made no mistake about you. The lady in the red cloak.'

# 8

Adam was waiting for her when she arrived at the Thistle Centre in Stirling. 'What is it, Cate? You look dreadful.' He put an arm round her shoulder.

She was clutching her cloak, wrapped in a plastic bag. She held it up for Adam to see.

'Good, let's put it into the cleaners now,' he said.

'Too late,' she almost choked on the words. 'It was in the boot of my car all morning, but it was still too late.'

He went very still. 'Why?'

And she told him about Yee Sung.

'How on earth did this impersonator know about the flyers? When did you deliver it to the printers?' he asked.

'I don't know how she knew. After we had lunch at the Pagoda I went to the newspaper office with the ad, then on to the printers with the flyer and poster originals,' she told him.

'You were wearing your cloak that day,' he reminded her.

Cate nodded. 'So she must have spotted me again, after impersonating me at the bank.'

'Exactly, and followed you. She must carry the cloak in a bag ready to impersonate you when the opportunity arises.'

'It was so easy to dress like me when she went into the printers to change the address on the publicity.' Cate felt sick with anger and frustration. 'At least the weekly paper doesn't come out for a couple of days. I'll check that she hasn't changed the address on the advertisement.'

She phoned the paper immediately on her mobile, but her impersonator hadn't visited them to alter the advertisement.' That, at least, was safe.

'I've asked the printer to supply me with new flyers and posters as soon as possible and I paid them extra for quick service. I don't think too many of the faulty ones have been distributed yet,' her voice was weary.

'I take it you checked with the printer about the person who had made the changes?'

Cate recounted the scene for him. She'd gone in directly after leaving the Café Felice. As usual, the printing office was humming not only with the machines, but the staff buzzing about. It was always a very busy place.

Cate said, 'Hello again.'

She was met with a polite smile. She put the faulty flyer on the counter. 'Do you remember me coming in to make alterations to this flyer?' she asked the person manning reception.

The girl shrugged. 'Sorry, we take turns to handle this counter.'

'So you don't remember my face?'

'Sorry,' the girl said again.

'Would you remember a person wearing a red cloak?'

'Oh her! Yeah, she came in the other day just before we closed. Said the original address on the flyer was wrong and asked us to change it.'

'OK,' Cate tried to sound casual. 'Only she got it wrong. The original address was the correct one. Can I ask you to print the flyers and posters again? I'll pay extra for twenty-four hour service.'

'No probs. Have you got a copy of the accurate one?'

Cate handed over her own original copy, together with a business card. 'Please don't make any alterations to this flyer without checking with me first. Ring me if anyone, especially someone wearing a red cloak, should come and attempt to alter anything.'

Adam listened to the story while gently shepherding Cate through the shopping mall to the dry cleaners.

'Did you mention to Yee Sung about your impersonator?'

Cate shook her head. 'Paola was there and I really didn't want to panic them. The downside is, of course, that I have probably lost Yee Sung's trust.'

'And what about Paola's trust?'

'Yes, I suppose I have to consider that too, although so far the only clients who have been targeted are long standing ones.'

'You mean they were on your books before Max left?'

'Yes,' she frowned. 'Do you think that's significant?'

'I don't know. It could just be coincidence, but now is the time to warn all your clients that someone is impersonating you. You've lost your two major clients and now you've had to pay to cover Yee Sung's losses. Paola could be next.'

They reached the dry cleaners and Cate handed over the red cloak. 'No hurry for it,' she told the assistant. 'I will probably ask my mother to collect it as I don't live in Stirling.'

If the assistant thought it was odd to leave an item when you didn't live in the area, she didn't question it.

'Actually,' Cate said as she and Adam left the shop. 'Now that I'm a bit calmer, I've a feeling that there was something out of place in the café. I just can't think what it was. You know how something jars, but unless you concentrate on it at the time, the significance fades away.'

'It goes into the memory bank. I've experienced that myself in my work,' Adam said. 'But it isn't lost. I just need a trigger to reactivate it. It will come, don't fret about it just now. Let it simmer and it will surface in time.'

'Thanks Adam.' She smiled at him. 'You are a great comfort to me. I think I might have gone under today if I hadn't had you to talk to.'

Adam wanted to be much more than 'a great comfort' to her, but he was wise enough to accept that until they got this fraudulent person out of her life, they could not move on in their personal relationship.

'By the way,' she went on. 'My parents and sister know nothing about the debt Max left me. Nor about anything that has happened over the last few weeks.'

'I'm not sure I agree with that,' he said.

She stopped in the street. 'You don't think they could be targeted?'

'Is your mother one of your clients?' he asked.

'Not as such. I do her accounting and tax returns, but she isn't on my client list. She insists on paying me by presenting me with paintings,' she said.

'But you do keep records of her business on your computer?'

'Oh heavens, yes!' she gasped. 'Is it possible that someone might have hacked into my computer?'

'We have to consider that a strong possibility,' he said.

'She's not going to get the better of me,' Cate said in a show of spirit.

'No, but now we fight in earnest. And for a start we need to alert your mother in some way, Cate,' he said as they approached the antique shop.

Mrs Lindsay beamed when she saw the pair enter her shop.

'Morning, Mum,' Cate kissed her

mother, trying to appear as relaxed as possible. 'You may remember meeting Adam the other day.'

'Of course, I do. How are you, Mr Stone?' Mrs Lindsay said.

'It's Adam, and I'm fine.' He smiled, shaking her hand.

'I was a bit uptight last time,' Cate said. 'As I'm sure you noticed. Adam and I had a disagreement.'

'All better now?' Mrs Lindsay teased.

'Yes, but it arose through something rather serious, Mum,' Cate said. 'Adam is actually Detective Inspector Stone from Ashrigg Police and he's helping me with a problem. Can we go into the back shop for a moment?'

Mrs Lindsay's eyes had widened with alarm, but she said nothing and led the way to the back shop.

Cate had decided to tell her mother the full story. She deserved nothing less, certainly if the impersonator should target her.

'My dear girl, how awful for you,' Mrs Lindsay said at the conclusion of

Cate's tale. She turned to Adam. 'I'm so glad you're with Cate, but what can I do to help?'

'First of all be on your guard. Cate tells me that you are not an official client, but at the moment your details are stored on her computer, so your business could still be vulnerable,' he said.

He then turned to Cate. 'I think we should transfer all your business records to my computer and close yours down until we have caught this person.'

'You mean the police computer?' Mrs Lindsay asked.

'No, that's not possible. I have a personal one at my home . . . I'm not going to give you my private address, not because I don't trust you Mrs Lindsay, but on the basis that the less people know it, the more secure it is.'

'Very sensible,' she pronounced.

'I don't think anyone is in any physical danger from this person,' he said. 'She is clearly out only to destroy

Cate's business.'

'But why? I can think of no-one in Ashrigg who is in the same line as me, who would need to poach my clients,' Cate said.

'Once we find out the 'why' then we will be much closer to finding her,' Adam said.

* * *

As they went to collect their cars, Adam said, 'I think it might be a good idea if you were to tell Erica everything. She is also another possible victim and as soon as we alert everybody the better.'

'Yes, I thought about her while we were in Mum's shop,' Cate said.

'She seemed to me to be a sharp cookie and not easy to con, but we can't tell how devious your impersonator is. I'm going into the office just to check on one or two things. Then we can meet at your flat, collect your computer and be at Owlsmoor as soon as we are free.'

Cate agreed, remembering she had keys to the cottage which she hadn't envisaged using. Still, things had changed now and she knew she was in great danger of losing her business entirely without Adam's help.

As she started the car and made for the main road back to Ashrigg, she accepted she had begun to trust him again. Maybe, of course, she'd never lost that, just mislaid it.

She had to wait patiently at Erica's pottery while her client dealt with some customers. Adam had said that whoever was impersonating must be of the same build and possibly colouring as herself.

The red cloak was a good identifying symbol, but not everyone would be taken in by it if the wearer didn't resemble Cate at least vaguely.

'I'm thinking of buying that Post Office that's been closed down near Croft Road,' Erica told her.

'Be absolutely sure everything is above board,' Cate said and then told her the whole story.

'Flaming Nora!' Erica thumped a ball of clay onto her worktable. 'That's unacceptable. Have you got rid of that cloak?'

'No, that would be giving in to her, but I have put it into the dry cleaners until she's caught,' she said.

'You are hoping to catch her?'

'With the help of a friend,' Cate said.

'The guy who was here same time as you the other day?' Erica grinned.

'How did you know?'

'Did you think I wouldn't spot the sidelong glances and the pair of you walking out together, speaking out of the sides of your mouths like Holly-wood gangsters?' Erica let out a shriek of laughter, then sobered up. 'He was checking me out, wasn't he?'

'Yes, sorry about that. He's a detective with the police.'

'Don't be sorry, it was the right thing to do. I came up clean, didn't I?'

'Of course.' Cate smiled. 'But you have to be on your guard. We're not sure if anyone has hacked into my computer, but I'm having all the information transferred this afternoon. It will soon be secure. But don't do anything which concerns money until you check with me first. You'll have to ring my mobile. I won't be home probably.'

Unexpectedly, Erica gave her a hug. 'I'm with you all the way, Cate. We'll get this blighter, sooner or later.'

* * *

Fortunately Adam's chief was in Ashrigg's headquarters when he arrived. 'It's the Cate Lindsay problem. Her impersonator has showed up again,' he said. 'She's definitely out to ruin Miss Lindsay and it's proving difficult to catch her.'

'We haven't the resources to help over this, especially as Miss Lindsay hasn't made any complaint to us officially,' his chief said.

'I know we have no evidence, no identification. Sergeant Paterson tells me there were no fingerprints on the bank slip or at the bank. The teller can't be sure, but he thinks she might have been wearing gloves. She kept her back to the video camera at all times.

'The teller has been shown a photograph of Cate, but he can't say if her impersonator resembled it or not. She evidently kept her head down all the time.'

'A professional then,' the chief said.

'That's my thinking and I want to ask your permission to use the computers here to see what I can find. It will be a case of just feeding some names in and seeing what comes up.'

'Sure, go ahead. Just don't charge me with overtime,' the Chief joked.

Adam knew his time was limited as he wanted to clear Cate's home computer as soon as possible. The impersonator must know by now that Cate had discovered about her trick at the printer's. She would be moving on to something else as fast as possible.

He ran as many checks as he could in

the time available. For the major one he had to approach someone else entirely. That could be done later.

* ★ *

When he arrived at Cate's flat, she had already switched off her computer. 'Everyone's files are now stored on a single DVD,' she said. 'All I need to do now is have my computer hard disk removed.'

'I'll do that.'

'Do you think she still might be following me?' Cate asked as he got to work on the computer.

'No, she can't be everywhere at once. She seems to restrict her movements to the Ashrigg area. She wants to ruin you, Cate, but she doesn't want to be caught.'

'She's had a lot of luck. I might well have gone to the bank after her that day. And the printer might have phoned me to double check on the changes in the publicity flyers and poster,' she pointed out.

'She's an opportunist, following you and impersonating you once she thinks you won't spot her. So far she's got away with it.'

'Anyway, just in case she's outside now, I don't want to take my car to Owlsmoor. That's your special place, your secret hideaway,' she said.

He grinned at her. 'It's secure. I got a bit of help from my chief when I told him what she'd been up to.'

'Such as?'

'Apart from letting me access the HOLMES computer in connection with your case, he's also provided transport — just for a couple of miles.'

Cate stared at him.

'Look out of your window. Do you see my car?' Cate got up from her desk and went to the window. Parked outside the block of flats was a police patrol car, complete with force logos and blue light.

'We'll leave in that together and it could look to anyone spying on you that you are being 'taken in'. My own car is parked a couple of miles away and we'll transfer to that and make our way to Owlsmoor.'

'Clever old you,' Cate said.

Once he'd removed her hard disk, they packed it together with her DVD, floppy disks and files and left her flat. Even if someone broke in they would find no information on her business.

Everything ran smoothly to plan and the constable driving the police car seemed highly amused at the subterfuge.

'First time I've seen a detective on the run,' he joked to Adam.

Once in the cottage, Adam and Cate got down to working out a strategy to inform all her clients. 'What you need is a code,' he told her. 'Advise all your clients that someone is trying to defraud you and they must not make any financial transactions without checking first with you, using a codename.'

'How about 'Piper',' Cate suggested.

Adam looked puzzled.

'The piper pays the tune. Clever?'

Adam smiled at her. 'It will do. It would take someone a long time to figure that one out. Also tell them to have no dealings with anyone wearing a red cloak.'

She printed out a note on Adam's computer and they decided to hand deliver a copy to each of her clients the following day.

'Could we start delivering these tonight?' she asked.

He shook his head. 'You will have to do this on your own — personally hand over this. Top security is the only way now.'

'Speaking of that, what did you mean by doing some checking on the police computer system?' she asked.

'I ran a check on all your major clients, just as a matter of form and, they all came up clean — bar one.'

Cate held her breath for a second. 'Who?'

'Have you remembered yet what

seemed out of place in the Café Felice this morning?' he asked.

Cate's stomach seemed to tilt. Not Yee Sung, not him!

'No,' she whispered.

'Well, Paola Trevi has probably never been near the Mediterranean. Our records show that she is one Polly Thomson from Merseyside.'

# 9

Adam arranged for a taxi to take Cate home. They were still being very cautious in case the impersonator had changed tactics.

Although there had been no repetition of the tender scene of her first visit to Owlsmoor, Cate felt very much at ease in his company again. She could tell that he was giving her time to recover from what she felt at the time had been a betrayal. She had now rationalised that in her mind.

She took her car next morning and personally visited every one of her clients, with only one exception, Paola Trevi, or Polly Thomson.

'Changing your name is not a crime,' Adam had assured Cate the previous evening. 'She did it legally so it is all above board. It probably was a good idea since she was opening an Italian café. The puzzling aspect is why she came to Ashrigg.'

'You said her last known address was some place in Merseyside.' Cate paused. 'Now I understand about her accent. Sometimes she didn't sound at all Italian, despite the broken English. I just assumed she spoke another language and I was hearing echoes of it.'

'So that's what was bothering you yesterday when she spoke with you and Yee Sung?' he asked.

'No,' she said at once. 'I'd noticed her accent before. It was something else and I still can't remember it. It's so frustrating.'

'I need to go back to the station in the morning to check on something,' he said. 'Let me be the one to warn Paola about your impersonator. I want to find out exactly why she chose a small town like Ashrigg for her café.'

'Are you suspicious of her? She's only been here for six months.'

'I'm suspicious of everyone.' He gave

her a tight smile. 'Goes with the territory.'

It was almost lunchtime before Cate reached Yee Sung. She handed over his new flyers and poster.

He bowed his thanks, but his eyes still looked worried.

She said she wanted to discuss an important matter with him and chose a corner table, away from the other customers. There she explained everything that had happened.

He was appalled. 'Cate, this is monstrous. You have lost customers and money! You paid twice for my flyers! This person must be stopped. What else can she do?'

'Adam is a Detective Inspector and although he can't officially deal with the case, he has been helping me,' she said. 'First of all, my client files have been removed from my computer, so no-one can access any. Secondly, you must only contact me by mobile phone and use the codeword 'Piper'. The last thing is, I'm sure I don't need to tell you, have nothing to do with any woman wearing a red cloak identical to mine. If you do see her, phone this number immediately.' She gave him one of Adam's police cards.

'You must warn Miss Trevi, too,' he said. 'She is the only one of your clients that I know.'

'Yes, that puzzled me a little,' she said. 'I have always kept my client files confidential and for the sake of security, tried to ensure that no-one knows about anyone else. How did she know you were my client?'

Yee Sung's eyes widened. 'She said she had seen you enter my restaurant. She recognised the red cloak.'

After leaving the Pagoda, she took the precaution of ringing Adam on his mobile to update him on Yee Sung's story.

'Thanks, Cate, that could be very significant. I'll play it by ear when I go to see her. I've received more information about your ex-business partner. I don't want to talk on the phone. I'll meet you at Yee Sung's once I've seen Paola.'

Cate had to be content with that as she set off again on the round of her clients, emphasising to each one that their accounts were no longer in any danger, but stressing the importance of the 'Piper' codeword and to keep an eye out for an impersonator in a red cloak.

Adam assembled all the information he had obtained over the last couple of days. It was going to come as a shock to Cate, but he was sure they were getting to the heart of the problem.

First, he'd enlisted his brother in Australia, a lawyer with good contacts. Colin had e-mailed the information that Australian Immigration in Sydney had no record of a Max Imrie entering the country within the last two years, or, for that matter, Martin Thomas, Michael Stanton, Maurice Williams.

Those were the names that had come up on the police computer — a man, with four names, wanted for fraud in

Merseyside. Max Imrie was a serial conman.

Adam was now convinced he was behind the victimisation of Cate, but he had no definite proof — nor had the other police forces involved in the previous scams. Only word of mouth from those he had defrauded, but of course each time he had disappeared before being caught. Only his names and crimes had appeared on record.

He'd taken his findings and proposals to the Chief and had been given permission to have Sergeant Paterson and Constable Anderson work with him that day.

Adam entered the Café Felice. It was busy; the two young girls were frenetically trying to deal with customers whlle a middle-aged woman was behind the counter attending to drinks and food orders.

At first he could not see Paola Trevi, then she suddenly appeared at the back of the café, shrugging off a jacket and taking a chair at a corner table. She had clearly been away from the café.

'Good morning, busy place.' He casually ambled over to her table and nodded to her.

'Buon giorno,' she greeted him with a flashing smile. He noticed a harshness behind the Italian greeting.

'I'd like to have a word with you. Business,' he said. 'It's about your account,' Adam said when they were seated.

Paola's eyebrows shot up. 'Cate Lindsay?'

Adam nodded. 'There has been a security breach with her clients' accounts,' he continued. 'I've come to warn you that your account might be in danger.'

Her brows contracted. 'Oh, that's bad news.' Then she gave him a hard stare. 'You work with her?'

Adam noticed the Italian accent had deserted her. 'No.' He took out his wallet and showed her his warrant card. 'I'm Inspector Stone of Ashrigg CID.'

Paola sat very still while Adam related each event that had involved the impersonator.

'Oh, how dreadful.' She opened her eyes wide as if to emphasise the drama and perhaps detract his attention from the tenseness in her voice. 'I heard that Yee Sung had problems with his publicity.'

'Yes, that was a nasty trick.' Adam smiled. 'But my main concern is the fraud that was perpetrated at the bank. That is a serious criminal offence and once we catch the person involved, it will result in a trial and possible prison sentence.'

Paola looked at him for a moment then suddenly snapped her fingers at one of the passing waitresses. 'Coffee for two, Tracy,' she said. It was a neat trick to give her time to think, Adam decided. But time too, for him to study her. She was approximately the same height and build as Cate and with a scarf round her head, concealing much of her face, could quite possibly pass for her.

He stood up. 'Thank you, Miss Trevi, but I don't have time for coffee. I just came to warn you about anyone impersonating Miss Lindsay and trying to gain details of your business.'

Outside, he saw Paterson gazing into the window of an expensive dress shop. Or so it appeared. She was actually watching him in its reflection. He gave her the briefest of nods. Constable Anderson was posted outside Paola Trevi's small terrace house not far from Cate's flat in Croft Road.

He would soon know every movement Paola made.

Cate had gone back to her flat to wait for Adam's call. While it had not lost its sense of comfort which she had so much enjoyed, she felt a little detached. This had been her home and office for a year now. Whatever happened in the future, she had decided she would find a small office for her work.

She wanted to keep the two areas of her life completely separate in future. When she'd come home last night, she'd phoned her sister and told her the whole story.

'You and the family are not in any danger,' she hastily reassured a horrified Sue. 'But just keep your eyes peeled for someone in a red cloak.'

'But I had that made specially for you!' her sister said.

'I know, but someone has been clever enough to copy it. Mum and Dad know what's happened and also that Adam is helping me. He's with the police.'

Adam called her soon after and she went straight to the Pagoda Restaurant.

As soon as they were seated at a table, Cate could contain herself no longer. 'Tell me about Max!'

'He is a serial conman,' Adam said. 'Wanted by the police in Merseyside. His modus operandi is to secure a position with a respectable accounting firm, then leave to set up his own business. He then poaches clients from that firm and in turn defrauds them. After that he promptly disappears.'

Cate was horrified. 'But he didn't defraud any of our clients.'

'Well, I reckon he discovered you

were too honest to be corrupted and so devised another plan.'

'To take the business away from me?' she asked.

Adam nodded. 'First of all, my brother checked and there is no record of Max entering Australia, let alone Sydney. I'm certain that he never left Scotland. When he walked out on you, he probably took copies of all the business dealings and would therefore have the account numbers of all your clients. Hence the fraud on the Dewars.'

'So my security wasn't breached.' Cate felt this was little comfort though.

'Exactly. It's my belief that he set up Paola in Ashrigg to be his accomplice on the spot. That wasn't until six months after he'd gone and you would suspect nothing.'

'He knew about my red cloak and so would be able to have a copy made for her. Presumably he sent the anonymous letters about the bad debt rumour to Howard Simpson and the Dewars.'

Cate saw the puzzle pieces fall into place.

'I reckon that's how it worked. The first impersonation — the kidnap hoax — was probably intended to bring you to the attention of the police, and also unsettle you so that your concentration would be lax.'

'And Paola disabled my car, to further upset me.'

Adam nodded. 'The bank fraud was a brilliant idea and had it come off, you would have lost all credibility with your clients.'

'It was just their bad luck that I was actually with a policeman when it happened.' She managed to smile at Adam.

'Paola made sure her staff actually ran the café, giving her time to leave it and follow you around.'

Cate thought for a moment. 'If I'd lost the business, Max would have moved in, telling everyone I was a walking disaster with faulty security and then he would have defrauded everyone.'

'That's his modus operandi,' Adam confirmed.

'You're sure about Paola?' she asked.

'She got a nasty shock this morning when she discovered I was a policeman. Also, I forgot to mention it the other day. She uses the name Polly Thomson as a stage name,' Adam said.

'She's an actress?' Cate was surprised.

'Small time, but good enough to impersonate you.'

'But why on earth would she team up with Max? How can she know him? She wasn't in Ashrigg when we were working together.'

Adam sighed. 'That's a mystery and somehow it doesn't seem to fit.'

'Max . . . and . . . Paola . . . I've remembered!' Cate burst out. 'That day in the café she called me Caterina. Only Max ever called me that!'

At that moment, his mobile rang. Adam listened carefully and Cate saw a smile slowly spread over his features.

'We've just got that bit of luck. I had

Paterson and McLean watching Paola,' he told Cate when the call was ended. 'They caught her trying to dispose of a red cloak, identical to yours.'

Cate actually felt sick. She had liked Paola and trusted her. The girl had thought nothing of trying to ruin her while affecting to be sympathetic and supportive.

'She's been taken to the police station. I'm going to interview her now,' Adam said.

★　★　★

When Adam entered the interview room, Paola was sitting in a chair trying to muster an air of defiance. On the table beside D.S. Paterson was a large evidence bag containing the red cloak.

'Do you want your solicitor present?' the sergeant asked.

'I don't have one in Ashrigg.' She shrugged carelessly.

'Do you have one in Merseyside, Polly Thomson?' Adam intervened.

Paola gasped, then shook her head violently.

D.S. Paterson then listed the occasions when Cate had been impersonated by a woman wearing a red cloak. 'This is yours?' She pointed to the evidence bag.

'Never seen it before,' Paola said.

'Come now, Paola, my sergeant and constable found you taking it from your house today,' Adam said.

She shrugged. 'Someone must have planted it.'

'We have the video from the bank on the day you tried to defraud the Flamingo sports club. You do realise that there is more than one video camera in the bank?' Adam said almost casually.

Paola's defiance evaporated at once. 'He told me if I kept my back to the video camera and wore gloves no-one would identify me or have my finger-prints!'

Adam made no comment. He certainly wasn't going to tell her that neither camera had provided a good enough

160

picture for identification. But Paola had fallen into his carefully laid trap.

'Who told you that?' he asked very softly.

Paola's mouth closed like a clam.

'You see, Paola,' Adam went on, 'We don't know who is behind this campaign to destroy Cate Lindsay. And it looks as if he — or she — might get away with it completely. You, on the other hand, won't. You will carry the can for the whole crime.'

Paola's face was white, but still she kept silent.

Adam gave a theatrical sigh. 'In that case, we will have to investigate all your known contacts in Merseyside. There are so many unsolved cases . . . '

'I wasn't involved in any of those!' she burst out. 'This is the first time he asked me.'

'Who?' Adam repeated softly. 'If I had a name, it might help your case.'

He watched as Paola fought with her conscience.

'Martin,' she muttered.

'Martin Thomas?' he asked.

'Yes.'

'Michael Stanton . . . Maurice Williams . . . And, of course, Max Imrie.'

'You knew all the time!' She snarled at him.

'No, I didn't. You actually gave the game away to Cate — quite inadvertently I might add.'

Paola was ashen. 'How?' she croaked.

'You called her Caterina. Only Max called her that. Tell us how you contact him,' Adam said. 'Tell us now! This man must be stopped before he causes any more harm.'

Paola didn't raise her head.

'You stand to lose everything, Paola — the café, your good name and above all, your freedom,' Adam said.

Slowly she lifted her head and looked at Adam. He saw the defeat in her eyes. 'I like the café. It was a good place. I wanted to stay on here. We thought it would all work out when Max took over again.'

'Did it not occur to you that he

might well have defrauded you, too?'

She shook her head violently. 'Never! We've known each other for a long time — back in Merseyside. He loves me!'

'He's been using you,' Adam said harshly. 'Unless we catch him, you'll never see him again. So how do you keep contact?'

She gave in quite suddenly. 'He phones me. Mobile.'

'I don't expect you use your real names for security. Have you a code?'

She nodded. 'Golden Fleece.'

How appropriate, Adam thought sourly. 'Where is he living?'

'Edinburgh.'

A big city, easy to hide in, Adam acknowledged. Without Paola's information they probably would not have a chance of catching him.

'When will he phone you?'

Paola pushed back her cuff and looked at her watch. 'Four-thirty. Same time every day, so I know it will be him.'

'OK, fifteen minutes to go. When he

calls, I want you to say that you have to meet. Problems have developed. Arrange a meeting place and tell him you will come wearing the red cloak as you don't want your real identity to be known.'

Paola looked sullen.

'You have no choice, Paola. Sergeant Paterson, please switch off the tape recorder. I'm going to take Miss Trevi to one of the other reception rooms.' He ushered Paola out of the interview room.

They went directly to the room where Cate was waiting. Paola shrank back when she saw her.

Cate said nothing, could not even look at Paola.

# 10

'Golden Fleece.' Paola spoke into her phone in a subdued voice. 'We need to meet, Max,' she said after listening for a moment. Adam and Cate could hear his voice as he snarled some words at Paola.

'Sorry, forgot. No names,' Paola said. 'There's a problem. I can't tell you over the phone.'

They noticed her hand gripping the receiver as she listened to Max's response. 'OK,' she said and immediately disconnected.

Adam leaned over and took the phone from her head. 'We can't allow you to communicate with him again, so I'll take charge of your phone.'

She looked at him, defeat in every line of her body. 'He wants us to meet tomorrow, around eleven o'clock in The Thistle Centre in Stirling, when it will be busy and no-one will notice us.'

'Good. That gives us time to set up an operation. You will wear the red cloak, Paola. He'll easily identify you and we can keep an eye on you. You will be quite safe,' Adam said.

'Max wouldn't touch me!' She flared with a brief anger.

'You are going to tell him that the scheme against Cate has been detected. He isn't going to be pleased about that to put it mildly. I agree that he had no record of violence, but this is the first time he's been unsuccessful with a scam,' Adam said.

'I don't have to tell him how you found out?' Paola had reverted to fear again.

'You won't have time,' Adam told her. 'Just a few words to him. I'll have an officer close by you, wired to record the words. You have confessed, you have named Max, we just want the visible proof of his guilt.' He turned and nodded at Sergeant Paterson. 'Take her away.'

'Come Miss Trevi. You will be spending the night in the cells.' Paterson had been leaning against the wall, watching the happenings. As she passed Cate on her way to collect Paola, she turned and looked directly at her.

Cate was surprised at the hesitation and then she saw the expression in Julie Paterson's eyes. It was a mixture of apology and regret. Cate knew it was entirely personal to her and she gave the sergeant a friendly nod in response.

After they left the room, she said to Adam: 'I want to be there tomorrow.'

He shook his head. 'No, Cate, not on the cards.'

'I'm not going to do anything rash. I just want to look once into Max Imrie's eyes when you've caught him.'

'You can't be part of the operation, you know that, but I certainly can't stop you being in the mall. But you didn't hear me say that.' He came over and lightly touched her arm.

Cate immediately covered his hand

with hers. 'I won't cause any trouble. I won't say a word. I just need to do this,' she said softly.

'I understand. Soon it will be all over.'

'Thanks, Adam, for everything,' she said.

'Catching Max Imrie is my job, the rest . . . ' He gazed at her for a long moment.

'For that too,' she murmured and knew her smile conveyed to him how her feelings had only been temporarily submerged by shock.

'I can't take you with me to Stirling tomorrow, I'm afraid you'll have to go under your steam,' he told her.

'No problem,' she said, a good idea just popping into her head.

'One thing puzzles me. Max is taking a chance going there. Doesn't he realise there is a possibility that he could be spotted by your parents?'

'He doesn't know they are there,' she told him. 'Mum didn't acquire her shop until just a few months ago, but I'll tell them to keep out of sight anyway until you've caught him.'

'Excellent. Once we've arrested him I'll have to bring him back here to Ashrigg, so why don't you return to your mother's shop and I'll collect you later. Maybe we could go on to Owlsmoor.'

She smiled at him. 'I still have my key for your cottage. Why don't I go straight there and have a meal ready for you.'

By now they were standing at the entrance to the police station. They were both longing to walk into each others' arms, but that certainly wasn't the place.

Adam placed a finger on Cate's lips. 'Until tomorrow,' he murmured.

As soon as she was home, Cate rang her parents. 'Can't say much yet, but don't leave the shop for any reason tomorrow morning. I'll pop in and see you first thing.'

She was there before her mother had even unlocked the door. 'Good heavens, Cate, you look like you've spent the night in those clothes. I hardly recognised you,' her mother was horrified.

'Good. Just the impression I want to make, but before anything else I need my dry cleaning ticket,' she assured her mother.

She left then and collected her cloak from the dry cleaners, although she had no intention of putting it on. Her rag bag selection of clothing — old jeans and sweater, ancient anorak and a pull-on woolly hat was her disguise. Or at least her temporary disguise.

★  ★  ★

Adam had his team in place as soon as the mall opened. Cate had given him a photograph of Max and this he'd had copied and distributed among the officers. They were all rigged out in plain clothes and looked like average shoppers.

'I don't trust Max Imrie in any respect,' Adam told the team. 'As we all know, once a con man, always one. And don't forget he's got away with every scam before this one. He may not think we're on to him, but he'll be very cagey.'

Around ten-thirty, he had sent Paola into the mall. He'd already provided her with a Debenham's bag and one from a pharmacy, just so that she didn't stand out from the crowd too much and also to hide her nervousness. She'd been instructed to window shop to keep her from studying every passer-by. Hovering close by and keeping a very watchful eye on her were Julie Paterson and another two female officers.

Max Imrie had not stipulated any exact place in his call to Paola so they really had to patrol all the avenues in the mall. Adam had left Paola's phone switched on overnight and noted there were two missed calls. Max had clearly tried to contact her again. The fact that she hadn't answered might alert him to trouble, but Adam was certain he'd be here to meet her.

Adam couldn't see Cate anywhere.

He knew she would do her best to keep out of sight. One glimpse of her and Max would be off like a shot.

Time dragged. Eleven o'clock came with no sign of Max Imrie. His team kept in touch by mobile — it looked most natural in the mall as every second person seemed to be using one. Paola was beginning to look very tense and restless, clearly finding the red cloak too warm to wear indoors.

Adam sat on one of the benches, a daily paper spread over his knees. He had a paper cup of coffee by his side and he took sips from it. Before long it was stone cold. Used as he was to similar stake-outs, he could feel the tension mounting.

At last his mobile rang. 'He's coming down your way, wearing track suit trousers, Barcelona football top and dirty trainers.' It was Cate's voice.

Horrified at her unidentified presence so close, he muttered, 'Get out of sight.' And cut the connection. Immediately he keyed Paterson's number and passed on the information. She'd guide Paola to this particular avenue and alert the rest of the team.

Cate's description was spot on, and Adam spotted Max when he was still a good few metres away. Three of his officers sent visual signals to Adam that they had him in their sights. They congregated together, laughing loudly and generally behaving in a loutish manner, all the time getting nearer and nearer to Max.

Just as the con man was about to pass him, Adam raised his newspaper but only so far. He could still see him over the top. At the same time, he spotted Paola and Julie approaching. They would collide with Max very soon.

Paola spotted Max and began to quicken her pace. Suddenly they were face to face. As if accidentally, Paterson dropped her own shopping bag beside Paola and made a delayed effort to retrieve it. She was bending down right by Paola's feet.

'The game's up, Max. We've been rumbled.'

Adam, now on his feet and moving in close, heard Max say, 'We can't be! Everything was running perfectly,' Max glared at Paola. 'You've done something stupid, haven't you? I had this all sewn up. Right, I'm out of here.' He was about to turn away when Paola grabbed him.

He tried to prise her hand from his arm. 'Watch me — and get rid of that cloak.' He gave her a push which sent her into Paterson's arms.

Before he could make another move, Adam and his team surrounded him, one officer swiftly handcuffing him.

Paterson formally arrested him and as they were about to take him away, they heard Cate's voice.

'Stop right there.'

Everyone, including Max turned round. Cate was standing in front of him, the woolly hat thrown off and her red cloak flung over her disreputable clothes.

Max's face which had contorted into a mask of fury, now seemed to fall apart at the sight of Cate.

She said nothing, just gave him a look of utter contempt and with a flick of her cloak turned and walked away.

*   *   *

'It's all over,' she told her parents when she returned to the antique shop. Both parents hugged her with relief and love.

She recounted the tale of Max never having gone to Sydney, but remaining in Scotland all the time. When Adam had conducted a second interview with Paola the previous evening, she told him that Max had found a job with a firm of reputable accountants in Edinburgh under yet another assumed name.

He planned to leave them once he'd secured Cate's clients and set up the business for himself. He reckoned that Cate would never be able to prove anything against him.

Adam had phoned Cate late that night with the new information. 'He would have committed the crimes all over again and all my clients would have lost everything.' She shivered at the thought.

'I never suspected Paola,' she now told her parents. 'I liked her, but she was blinkered about Max too. It seems she was aware of some of his past history and only agreed to come to Ashrigg and open the café as a cover for him. He had agreed to pay her well. As a struggling actress she was always chronically short of money.'

'And not too particular how she earned it,' Cate's father said dryly. 'Your problem, my child, is that you are too trusting of everyone.'

'I'm sorry that she will be charged as an accessory over this, but she did have a choice. And she betrayed me,' Cate paused for a moment. 'I don't want to become cynical about people, but it has been a hard lesson for me.'

'It might also be a warning to you not

to be so independent and proud in future,' her father said. 'You know we would have helped out financially.'

'Yes, of course, but I felt so foolish about being deceived by Max.'

'He's out of your life now,' her mother said and dismissed him. She took a deep breath. 'Now, this charming Adam — why don't you ask him over here and we'll have a celebration.'

'Thanks, Mum, but can we take a raincheck on that?' Cate smiled, concealing her amusement at her mother's blatant tactics.

The ever smart Mrs Lindsay pounced on the *we*. 'So is the wind blowing that way?'

Cate laughed. 'Wait and see. But the celebration tonight is just for Adam and me.'

'Hmm, at that secret cottage I'll be bound.' She smiled coyly.

'I'm going home now to change,' Cate said, refusing to be drawn.

'I should think so too! That's hardly a romantic outfit,' her mother said.

Cate found once she was home that she was completely exhausted. She guessed it was more from stress than any physical cause. Briefly she relived that moment when she'd looked Max in the eye!

It was the first time that he'd had to face someone he'd tried to cheat. He'd run off before all his previous victims had realised what he'd done.

That moment in the mall she saw the real man behind the suave, hypocritical mask. She felt no sympathy for him. He deserved all that he was going to get.

It wasn't personal, with Adam's help she had outwitted him, but her concerns were for those earlier victims who had probably lost all their savings.

Now she and her clients were safe from his predatory crime. She thought of phoning them to confirm that the crisis was over. But then she paused. She had been truthful when she'd told her parents the events would not make her cynical, but from now on she would be wary. Perhaps it was a good idea just to let the safety code stay in place.

Anyway, for the first time in a year her clients were not her top priority. Adam was. What a difference in the two men. Adam — loyal, steadfast, a man of integrity, a man who cared about human life. All the attributes she admired. Added to that was his warmth and . . . well, there was lots more she had to learn about him.

She didn't know if they would have a future together, but she knew she wouldn't find anyone as fine again.

She jumped up from the sofa, threw off the worn clothes that had provided such a good disguise and took a shower. Then she rushed out to the supermarket — the very one where all the drama had begun and bought some fine ingredients for a celebratory meal, plus champagne, candles, flowers, chocolates, all the while her heart singing.

Back in the flat again, she chose a flounced and frilled skirt she'd never had a chance to wear, teamed it with a floaty blouse plus some of her favourite jewellery, and added the finishing touch of a splash of her special perfume.

She loaded her car and set off for Owlsmoor.

She had no idea when Adam would arrive. Max would have to be questioned, the case tightly sewn up and then there was Paola, the accessory to deal with too. Cate firmly put them out of her mind.

The meal took time as she was determined it would be perfect. A goats' cheese starter, a main course of sea bass with a tricky sauce and delicately prepared vegetables and to finish her favourite dessert — a compote of yogurt, cream, walnuts and honey.

The champagne was chilled, as was the white wine, the red uncorked and breathing. The table was laid and matches waiting beside the candles. As soon as she heard his car she'd light them. The open fire was already blazing nicely.

Time passed, but the anticipation of

his arrival kept her spirits up. Besides, she felt enveloped in the peaceful atmosphere of the cottage and had time now to assimilate the beauty of his home.

At last she heard the hum of a car engine. She went to open the door and stood there as Adam got out of his car.

She had no idea that the soft firelight illuminated her from behind and that Adam saw his love framed in a soft glow that slowly drew him towards her. She held out her hands to welcome him, not only to his home but to her heart.

He walked towards her, reaching for her. She was all that he had ever wanted.

## THE END

## LOOKING FOR LOVE

### Zelma Falkiner

Fleur's sweetheart, Tom, disappeared after being conscripted into the Army during the Vietnam War. Twenty years later, Fleur finds a package of his unread letters, intercepted and hidden by her widowed mother. From them, she learns that he felt betrayed by her silence. Dismayed, but determined to explain, Fleur engages Lucas, a private investigator, to help in the search that takes them to Vietnam. Will she find Tom there and put right the wrong?

# RELUCTANT DESIRE

## Kay Gregory

Laura was furious. It was bad enough having to share her home with a stranger for a month — but being forced to live under the same roof as the notorious Adam Veryan . . . His midnight-dark eyes challenged Laura to forget about her fiancé Rodney, and she knew instinctively that Adam would be a dangerous, disruptive presence in her life. She'd be a fool to surrender her heart to such careless custody . . . but could she resist Adam's flirtatious charm?

# CHANCE ENCOUNTER

## Shirley Heaton

When her fiancé cancels their forthcoming wedding, Sophie books a holiday in Spain to overcome her disappointment. After wrongly accusing a stranger, Matt, of taking her suitcase at the airport, she is embarrassed to find he is staying at her hotel. When she discovers a mysterious package inside her suitcase, she suspects that the package is linked to him. But then she finds herself falling in love with Matt — and, after a series of mysterious encounters, she is filled with doubts . . .

# KIWI SUNSET

## Maureen Stephenson

In 1869, dismissed from her employment with Lady Howarth after being falsely accused of stealing, Mairin Houlihan emigrates to New Zealand. There she meets Marcus, the son of Lady Howarth, who had emigrated there to farm sheep. But later, despite her innocence, Mairin is held on remand on suspicion of murder. Marcus tries to help her — but with all the circumstantial evidence against her, how can he? If convicted she will hang. Who had committed this terrible murder?